How
Guy i.. ..

JANE LINFOOT

Harper impulse
we've got the love

Harper*Impulse* an imprint of
HarperCollins*Publishers Ltd*
77–85 Fulham Palace Road
Hammersmith, London W6 8JB

www.harpercollins.co.uk

A Paperback Original 2013

First published in Great Britain in ebook format by HarperImpulse 2013

A catalogue record for this book
is available from the British Library

ISBN: 978-0-00-755963-3

Automatically produced by Atomik ePublisher from Easypress

CHAPTER ONE

'SO, how's things?'

Ed Mitchum turned to see his sister, Cassie, swirling towards him across the lawn. She dropped a fizzing glass into his hand as she came to a halt beside him.

'Mineral water?' He surveyed the floating lemon slice with distaste, took in her inscrutable nod, and snatched a glass of champagne in his other hand from a passing waiter, before she had time to protest. 'Much as I appreciate your concern for my well-being, your assumption that it's fine to interfere in my life-choices is getting damned annoying. You're in danger of taking the bossy sister thing too far.'

She spun a dazzling smile up at him and tossed her sea of platinum curls over one shoulder. 'Okay, keep your hair on! I just don't think it's appropriate for you to drink yourself under the table at the Olds' anniversary party, that's all. I'd hoped you'd bring Sophie today. Couldn't she make it?'

'Sophie....?' Ed racked his brains, and failed to come up with a face to fit the name.

'As in dark, gorgeous, legs the length of Park Lane – pretty much surgically attached to you at the Carlton's tennis and Pimms do?'

'Ahhh, *her*. Ancient history, I'm afraid.' Cassie's incensed expression only served to spur him on. 'Keep up! There's been several since – what was she called again? Not that the women or my alcohol consumption have anything to do with you.'

Cassie let out an infuriated sigh. 'It's only because we care, isn't it Will?'

She tilted her head, appealing to his best friend Will, who had just arrived at her elbow, and was wilting visibly under the full glare of her sudden smile.

'Leave Will out of this.' Ed grimaced as Will's scowl over Cassie's head reminded him of the animosity between his best friend and his seriously annoying younger sister. Cassie had taken great pleasure in driving Will to distraction since the first day Ed had brought him home, aged eleven. Twenty years of torment later, they were still sparking off each other... not in a good way.

'It's time you grew up if you ask me.' Cassie smirked at him. 'And I'm not just talking about your drinking habits. Seriously Ed, you're pushing thirty two. Isn't it time you were settling down?'

An over-bearing sister who thought she knew it all. When in reality the woman hadn't got the first idea. Settling down was the last thing on his mind, although now she'd mentioned coupling, a party pick-up was no bad idea. On the lookout for a likely candidate, he scanned the neat lawns as far as the distant walls of his parents Derbyshire castle until his gaze snagged on a glossy brunette with a perfect bob, whose sheer sheath of a dress was split to the hip.

Cassie was onto him in a nano-second. 'Pointless looking there, Ed, that's Uncle Henry's latest wife. I know he never keeps them long, but this one's new enough to make it through to the end of the party.'

'I wouldn't bank on it.' Ed sent her a sardonic smile. 'Not if the way she's eyeing up the blonde Adonis waiter is anything to go by. She practically licked him as he passed.'

Will posted him a lazy wink. 'For a man who specialises in

4

blowing things up, you've been remarkably quiet lately. How *is* your love life these days? Bed still like a conveyor belt?'

Ed shrugged. 'Can't complain. Turn-over's still satisfyingly high.'

'Well I'm sure you're going to make plenty of noise with your firework display this evening. You get some points back for doing that.' Cassie's face softened to a smile, before she whirled on him again, piercing him with her sky-blue eyes. 'So why don't you keep any these women of yours?'

For a fleeting moment he shrank under the ferocity of her scrutiny. Then remembering it was none of her damned business anyway, he relaxed.

'If you must know, when it comes to it, they never hold my interest. One night and I've seen all they have to offer. Two max. Then I'm all ready for the next.'

'Perhaps you're dating the wrong kind of woman.' Cassie said.

'Meaning?'

Ed saw Will narrow his eyes at Cassie, warning her. With Cassie in full force a guy needed his wingman.

'I'm not backing off here, Will.' She sounded fierce. 'Ed's always surrounded by women, hoards of them. All desperate to jump onto his love conveyor-belt, all desperate to be the one who gets to hang on in there. But let's face it, you are a great looking guy with an even greater personality when you want to be, but those women have got their eye on the contents of your wallet more than on your personal attributes. And their desperation to get their hooks into you, and gain access to your billions must make them much more compliant than they otherwise might be. And in my book, compliant equals boring. Be honest Ed, when did you last date a woman who challenged you?'

Ed opened his mouth to answer then shut it again when he couldn't remember an instance.

'These polished, high maintenance females, solely attracted to your bank-balance, can't give you more than one night of distraction. It's obvious.'

'You talk about it as if I even give a damn.' He shot her a pointed grin. 'I don't. I'm happy with things as they are.'

'You tell him Will. You're his oldest friend after all.'

Cassie appealing to Will? Again? Twice in the course of two minutes.

'She might have a point.' Will's tone was measured. He threw in a conciliatory qualifier. 'Maybe.'

Now that was an unlikely alliance.

Ed swallowed his distaste. 'How you two have both survived a decade of serial monogamy without dying of boredom is beyond me, but seeing as you are setting yourselves up as experts here, what do you suggest?'

He hesitated, waited for their responses, which weren't as immediate as he'd expected, and seized on their silence. 'There, not so easy is it?'

Cassie tapped her teeth with one crimson nail as she thought. 'This isn't something we can rush. It's too important for that. For starters, I'm thinking you need to choose someone who has no idea you have money. And you need to see her more than twice – give yourself a chance to get to know her properly.'

Ed squirmed. 'I think I liked you better when you were telling me not to drink so much.'

Will chimed in, 'Think of it as a challenge. We can add in some motivators, obviously.'

Motivators? Just like Will to know how to make him bite.

'I haven't agreed to this.' It was important to protest, but as soon as Ed heard the word 'challenge', he knew he was in. It would shut them up and get them off his back once and for all. Then afterwards the only person he had to please was himself.

Will rubbed his hands. 'So, down to business. Let's say ten dates?'

He wrinkled his forehead as he thought. 'To include at least two nights away – the wonders of the mini-break and all that.'

'Ten?' Ed felt his jaw drop.

'If you're going to do it, you may as well do it properly.' Cassie flapped her hands in excited anticipation.

'And you mustn't reveal how much you're worth....' Will added.

'Or use luxury props or enticements.' Cassie said quickly. 'And no sex on the first date.'

Ed shook his head in protest. 'Hang on; I draw the line at that.'

'Fine, whatever, but if you've got any sense you'll keep to that anyway.' Cassie grinned at him. 'Even if you don't meet the love of your life with this, you might improve your dating habits. Though frankly they don't sound like they could get any worse.'

'Don't be so sure. I always practise safe sex.' He flashed her a smirk.

'There will have to be sex at some stage, or it won't count either.' Cassie was quickly getting carried away. 'And we need to meet her on one of the dates, and it would be good for you to meet her family too.'

'No pressure there then?' Ed raised his eyebrows. This was in danger of getting out of hand. 'So before Cassie adds in any more clauses, what about the carrot, Will? What are you offering?'

'It'll have to be good. What do I have that you've always coveted? My first-edition *Definitely, Maybe* album? Yours, if you complete the challenge, regardless of the outcome?'

'You know you can do better than that, Will.'

'Okay. Throw in the ski lodge in Klosters too, if you must. It'd be good to know it's in safe hands with you. Might make you take a holiday at last.'

'Great, you're on. And the stick will be that if I fail to complete, I'll give you my Jarvis Cocker signed T-shirt.'

'Add in your Edinburgh town house, and we have a deal. I fancy the idea of wearing a kilt.'

'Fair enough. Though there's no risk you'll be getting it – I'll manage ten dates with my eyes closed. And one last thing… A measure of how confident I am that this whole stunt will ultimately fail.' Ed swayed back on his heels, and locked eyes with Will. 'If I find a woman I fall in love with, I'm ready to gift you my vintage Aston Martin.'

'But come on, you'd never give that up!' Cassie looked shocked.

'Exactly!' His face split into the widest smile. 'There's absolutely no danger that I'm going to have to!'

***

'All set?'

A bright Monday morning, one month later, Ed kicked a foot in the dust as he waited. Digging his hands into his pockets, he stared around the quarry, wondering when he became so removed from the place where he'd had his first taste of the explosions – a taste that had turned into a lifetime obsession. He'd promised the quarry Manager, Blake he'd be here today, when they'd met up at his parents' party, and he didn't like to let Blake down. Not after everything Blake had done for him, in those bad old days when Ed was fourteen and a hell-raiser.

'Ready to go.' Blake gave him a nod. 'Jeans and tee okay for you? Sorry, but they're the best I could muster from the lads. This is Derbyshire, not London, remember.'

'My fault I ripped the sump of the car then proceeded to smear the contents all over myself. I'll take what I can get.' Ed gave a rueful grin, as he looked down at the indecently tight jeans complete with rips, and the saggy, beyond-hope t-shirt someone had donated to his cause. He exhaled deeply, as he glanced at his shiny sports car, waiting for the recovery vehicle by the gate. He, of all people, should have known better. Would have known better if he'd been half-way concentrating, instead of raging because a month into this Dating Challenge, he still hadn't found a suitable woman. Damn his sister and her determination to make sure the whole world paired up into happy couples. If he hadn't been fuming about the Coupledom Challenge, instead of looking out for ruts in the ground, he'd still have a working car. He'd have to make do with the quarry Land Rover until a replacement arrived.

'I feel like we should be smashing bottles of champagne against the cliffs, given all the effort we've put into getting the permissions to extend the quarry. I guess we'll have just have to make do with the big bang instead,' Ed said, a grin of anticipation playing on his lips. 'Whenever you're ready.'

However many explosions he saw, he never tired of the thrill of a good blast. Ten years in the boardroom and yet the warning siren's wail still sent prickles across the back of his neck as he trained his eyes on the rock face. Then in the split second before the blast, a rider on a horse cut across the skyline, up behind the blast area.

What the hell? There shouldn't be anyone up there!

Then the boom of the blast smacked against his body, and he heard the echoing thud as the rock-face collapsed. But Ed wasn't watching the falling rock. Because above it, the horse was jack-knifing into the air. Against the backdrop of the perfect blue sky Ed watched transfixed, as the horse and rider separated, and the rider tumbled downwards, out of view. Then the dust rose, in billowing rolls over the rock-pile, and just before the dust haze turned the blue sky grey, he saw the rider less horse galloping against the horizon.

'There's a problem in the field up there! Damned stupid riders.' Ed hurled himself in the direction of the Land Rover, grinding his teeth on grit.

Within seconds he was roaring towards the quarry gate, powered by a whole mountain of wrath. He was still cursing, minutes later, up in the field, as he jumped down beside the casualty.

A girl. And the fact she'd left her riding hat on the gatepost suggested she had no brains to protect. A blonde, albeit a dirty one. Spread-eagled on the grass. In tiny shorts, and with curvy, honeyed legs, that sent crackles up his spine and made him remind himself he shouldn't be noticing.

His eye snagged on the tendrils of a tattoo that emerged from the top of her boot.

'Can you hear me?' The anger drained from him as he waited for her reply. He made the words clear. 'I'm Ed, I'm here to help. What's your name?' He was going through the routine now, and she damned well wasn't responding. No chance of ringing for an ambulance either, the way the signal was here.

She was very still, face to the sky, blanched beneath her freckled tan. He shivered as he saw blood on the grass, already matting in the tangled strands of her hair, his heart banging, as his training kicked in.

Airways, breathing, circulation.

Bearing in mind not to move her spine, he squatted beside her, and grasped her wrist, wincing at the tightness of his on-loan jeans. Tried not to notice that she smelled of flowers. Vanilla. Warmth. Woman.

Nothing. Damn. He was always crap at finding a pulse. He dragged her hair aside, tried again. This time two fingers under her jaw found firm flesh, slightly clammy, but still no pulse.

He put his cheek to her slightly parted lips. Waited a second to see if she was breathing.

Nothing.

Ninety nine percent sure she was just unconscious, her lack of pulse was down to his lousy technique at locating it, and not because she was dead. But what the hell should he do now? He couldn't just stand here and do nothing. He stood up, ran his eyes down the length of her, his brain struggling to remember his first aid training. Whether to go for her chest first, where one top button had pulled undone, and, let's be honest, he might never find a breastbone. Or her mouth.

It was never like this on the first-aid dummies.

He was on his knees now, sizing up lips that were lush, soft, parted, but altogether easier than the alternative. He needed to damn well get on with it before he ran out of time.

Focusing on the graze of mud on her cheek, he nipped her nostrils, grasped her chin. He drew in one long breath through his nose, clamped his mouth over hers and psyched himself up to blow.

Wallop!

One arm flopped up and clamped the back of his head. Then her other landed square on his back.

What the hell?

Her tongue feathered his for a moment, and then came in for the kill, as his already thumping heart exploded in his chest. He fought to pull away but she had him in a head lock, exploring, tangling with him. Drawing him in.

Salty. Gritty. Entirely off limits. And then, in sheer relief that she was alive, he was kissing her back, an ocean-rush of blood hammering in his ears, his whole body on adrenalin-surge, endorphin-pumping, red-alert. Hotter than he could say. Knowing it was out and out wrong, hearing the gentle moans in her throat, but nothing he could do.

Except go with it.

***

Millie Brown was drifting, and dreaming, a thing she tried her best not to do. Even in her sleep, she liked to stay in control, and largely she managed to keep her sleeping mind a blank. But something odd had happened, and she was plunging headlong into a full-on sexy-scenario dream she was powerless to stop.

Right now, a guy with a voice like dark chocolate, was capturing her mouth, and tasting delicious. Cappuccino and hot, raw man. Definitely not love-rat-of-the-decade ex, Josh, then. Who she definitely was over, wasn't she? No, this was a guy who could really kiss. Talk about tongues and technique. Two years without a snog, but she still knew a high quality kiss when it hit her. And he was ramping it up. In for the kill, and boy, she was happy to die and fast-forward to heaven. Heaven was definitely where she'd arrived, as she shifted beneath him, heard herself moan in the distance, aching for more amazing. Even the sting of his stubble on her chin was delectable. Could almost be....

Real?

Slowly, she slid her fingers through the strands of his hair, traced them across the alarmingly tangible thrust of his cheekbone, and brought her palm to rest on a rough jaw that sent tingles up her arm. Horribly real tingles.

She opened her eyes. Blinked. Blinked again.

Awwww crap! Her stomach squelched, and her heart did one huge squeeze, then started to hammer, as the very real man who was kissing her tore his face away from hers.

She put a hand to her mouth. Found the hottest kiss ever had morphed into a gaping chasm. And as her eyes finally pulled into focus she heard that chocolate voice again.

'Welcome back, Sleeping Beauty!'

Millie struggled to catch her breath.

'Pleased to see you're not dead then.' He'd shot backwards, and was towering over her now, face like a storm cloud. 'And I think

12

we can safely say your arms aren't broken, given the strength of your grip on my neck.'

Millie rubbed a hand across her bottom lip, tried to make sense of what she was doing here, and gawped at the vision of glorious manhood before her. Dark, choppy hair, jeans like a second skin that underlined the solid power of the guy. Dusty work boots that hollered rough and ready. A ragged t-shirt that screamed don't-give-a-damn, or up-for-anything, she wasn't sure which. And this is what she'd woken up snogging? If ever there was sex on legs, this had to be it.

'What just happened?' She clasped a palm to her throbbing skull as she tried to piece together fragments of how she got here. 'I was riding up the hill in the field...'

Exercising Cracker, the pony. Thinking how her legs were so tanned they looked like they weren't hers, how she wouldn't need the tanning salon this year, how that was the only good thing about living in the country.

'And I was humming 'Leave your hat on'...' Going through the Burlesque routine she'd been working on earlier this morning, for her up-coming workshop. Singing the tune. Trying to plan out the next bit of the sequence in her head as she rode. 'Then there was this bang.'

The pony surging beneath her in panic, the ground whizzing towards her, the slam of her skull as it whacked into the ground. She definitely remembered that.

'Humming 'Leave your hat on'? Ironic choice then.' He gave a snort. 'We were blasting in the quarry, and your horse took off. I assume you fell and hit your head. You were out cold when I found you.'

'So what was that back there, the kiss of life?' She fixed him with a fierce stare, which dwindled as she relived how darned amazing he'd tasted. And smelled. Still did. She caught a waft of him on the breeze, and fought a sudden desire to seize his leg and bury her face in it.

His mouth twisted into a wry line. 'Something like that.'

'Don't you know it's wrong to take advantage in situations like this?' She pushed herself up on her elbows, hurled the accusation at him, and winced at the pain which split through her head.

'Hang on! Let's get this straight. *You* were the one who got *me* in a headlock as you came around.' He stood his ground, indignant and glowering. 'I began resuscitation when I couldn't find a pulse and you didn't appear to be breathing, then what do I know, you've jumped me! Apologies for trying to save your life. Next time I won't bother.' He made a dive for his Land Rover.

She'd been the one snogging the socks off him?

So that was what two years giving guys a wide berth did to you. Made you into a sex fiend when you were unconscious. Her body shuddered, shriveling in a giant cringe of embarrassment. She pushed herself up to sit and another spear of pain crashed through her skull.

'Let me see your head. You shouldn't have been here on a horse you know, it's private land, and it's not a bridleway.' He'd come back from the Land Rover with bandages, a ready-made lecture, and a double dose of bad mood. At least that covered her shame. He was leaning behind her now sounding seriously snappy as he prodded in her hair.

'You've got a nasty gash, probably hit a stone, but the bleeding's not too bad. Hold this dressing whilst I fix it. One head injury, which would have been avoided had your riding hat been protecting you, not the gatepost.'

Short tempered. Snarky. Not attractive. Except he was. Devastatingly.

'Ouch, there's no need to manhandle me!'

And rough too, as he crashed the bandage into place, taking

control. Making her spine zither like crazy. Though he did have a point about her hat. Leaving it on the gatepost was one bad decision.

'You need to go to casualty.'

'No way!' Casualty was the last place on earth she wanted to go.

'I'll run you there, or you can wait for an ambulance. Your choice. Whichever way, hospital is where you're going.' He backed away, stood like a dictator, legs splayed, practically bursting out of that faded denim in every area that mattered.

So, she may have a head injury, she may be dying of embarrassment, but she couldn't let this power-house of a guy take over.

'I can't go anywhere until I've sorted the pony out. It's my job to look after him, and my house depends on my job, and if I lose my house it'll blow my whole life-plan out of the water.' She hugged her knees tight, instantly regretting the personal information spill. Luckily he seemed oblivious.

'For crying out loud! The pony's up there, in the corner of the field, grazing, looking a darned sight better than you. I'll get Blake from the quarry to sort him out. He knows about ponies.'

Now for the biggie. She screwed herself up to force it out. 'But I don't do hospitals...'

One small voice protest she might as well not have made, judging by his sneer.

'Well in that case you should have taken better care not to rip a hole in your head!' He sighed. 'Jeez, how difficult can you make this? Can you stand up?'

He stuck out a hand in her direction. Broad, oil-streaked. She considered refusing it. Then thought again. His strong fist enveloped hers, and with one brutal tug she was on her feet, thumping into the bolster of his body, looking up at a star shaped scar on the underside of his chin.

'Good work.'

Another tug, and she was half way to the Land Rover, and he'd flung the door wide. The next moment he'd shouldered her up into the seat and fixed her with a stony glare.

'Okay. No nonsense. No jumping out. And if you're going to throw up for goodness sake then shout. I'm Ed Mitchum by the way. I work for Quarry Holdings.'

Hadn't he already told her that? She replied through gritted teeth. 'Millie Brown. Pleased to meet you.' *Not.*

Too late. He'd already slammed the door.

CHAPTER TWO

'COULD you please make the smallest effort to sit still, or do I have to watch you wriggle in your seat all day?' Ed's voice echoed off the walls of the hospital waiting area, short, gruff, tetchy.

Millie sent him a searing scowl. He was making no effort to hide his irritation, so why should she. With his stubble shadow, and his denim rips he seemed too large and blatantly sexual for this clean, clinical environment. Too bad this was all taking so long.

Waiting was the name of the game here, and irritated as he sounded, he was much better at waiting than she was, sitting all chilled and relaxed, one well-muscled arm flung across the back of the next chair, whilst she changed position once a second.

She'd already been into a cubicle with a nurse and answered lots of questions.

Name? Millie Brown, aka.... no need to expand on that one. Headache? Yeah, obviously. Double vision? Not yet, except perhaps when she went cross eyed ogling the hunk that brought her here. Mental note to self to stop that. Drowsy? No more than usual. Dizzy? Not that she was admitting it, and only because the whole A&E thing was making her hyperventilate. One glimpse of a blue surgical gown was enough to spin her right back to that last awful time she'd been in hospital. The panic she'd felt, then the pain, and the desperate emptiness afterwards. The smell of the antiseptic took the blurry images and brought them back in Technicolor. So much so, that when she'd gone to another room where another nurse stuck her cut together with glue, the nurse made her lie down before she let her go back to the waiting area.

And sitting with *him* now was driving her further up the wall than ever. Every time she saw him her mind went off on its own out-of-control extrapolation, along the lines of rocks, wet skin, underwear, sex, for no other good reason than because the guy had emerged from the quarry, looking like a model who'd lost the fashion shoot. It was bad enough being here – the smell of the place was making her feel faint – without having this Ed and his whole heap of attitude along for the ride.

She leaned towards him. 'You really don't need to stay. At this rate, it may take all day. I'll be fine on my own, thanks.'

'And you'll get home how?' His long, lean legs extended towards her as he stretched, and crossed his ankles casually.

She pursed her lips, screwed up her face, and refused to look at the straining denim bulge at his groin. He had her there. She had no money on her. No phone. The hospital was miles away from home. If she had to get a taxi back, it would cost an arm and a leg, and there was no-one she could think of to ring to collect her. One bad idea to end up here when her best friend was away. So much for being independent. She let that one go.

'You could go for a coffee or something?' Give her a break from his shed-loads of animal magnetism.

'And they might move you in the meantime. Given that your phone is lying up in that field, I might never find you again.'

No answer to that one either. She watched him stand up, ease back those disgustingly broad shoulders, and saunter towards a table of magazines. Only because there wasn't anything else to look at. Nothing to do with the fact he was eye-candy of the highest order. Sweet as it came.

And one heck of a kisser.

That much she could remember. Even if it had been an accident. Her eyelids fluttered involuntarily and her mouth watered at the thought of it. The taste. She jumped as he burst in on her action re-play.

'Want a magazine?' He held up a copy of Ideal Home. 'Horse and Hound? Hello? Woman's Weekly?'

She shook her head, and prayed she hadn't flushed as fuchsia pink as she felt. And the tilt of his head said he was mocking her too. Damn. Shame he didn't have a personality to match the looks and the kissing skills. Shame for someone, though not her, obviously. Men were nowhere on her agenda, not even on the distant horizon. Definitely no room for a drop dead specimen who'd materialized from nowhere to pay havoc with her pulse rate. Not with her life-plan.

Her eyes were still glued to him as he sat down and open a dog-eared car magazine. It was so unfair when a man got eyelashes like that. Thick, delectably dark. At least Motor World might keep him off her case.

'Millie Brown?' Millie started as she heard an approaching nurse shout her name. 'The doctor wants you to go down to X-ray. There may be quite a wait.'

'X-ray?' Millie felt her chin jut defensively, as her chest tightened. 'Why do I need an X-ray?'

'How about, to see if you've got a cracked skull?'

Arrogant Ed got in before the nurse, who wafted a sheaf of papers at Ed, then winked at Mille. 'We'll let your partner take charge of the papers. Make sure he looks after you!'

Millie opened her mouth to protest loud and hard, but the nurse had already bustled away.

'That's official, then. I'm along for the ride.' Ed shot her a satisfied smirk. 'Do you want to take Horse and Hound with you? And

19

do you want to go in a wheelchair, or on a trolley?'

***

X-ray was a marathon away. At least.

From her milky pallor, Ed would have laid a bet that Miss Independence here was regretting refusing transport, but if she was stubborn and belligerent, that was down to her. When they finally reached X-ray it was after a series of false starts, wrong turns, and a whole heap of silent recriminations, on both sides.

'Grab a seat. I'll sort the official stuff.' He sidled up to reception, doubting that Millie had the strength to stand. Confidently, he threw the receptionist the full-on radiance of the five hundred watt smile he kept for emergency use only and was sent away with a promise of a two hour wait. Without the smile he suspected it could have been two weeks.

Millie gave the bloodstained haystack of hair above the bandage a vigorous rub, and groaned loudly as he landed on the seat next to her. 'I just lost the will to live.'

She leaned back on her plastic chair and closed her eyes.

Was she really that stupid? 'I thought they told you not to go to sleep.'

She blew loudly, opened her eyes and flashed him a flaming stare. 'I'm not. Okay?'

Then promptly shut her eyes again.

Something about the undiluted indignation in the angle of her chin made him smile. Hell, he should've sent Blake to do this, or one of the other guys. There was no need for him to be here. The details of the firework display in Provence still had to be finalised, there were company takeovers that needed his attention, but for one strange moment he didn't mind being here at all. Possibly

20

he was feeling guilty that the old warning signs up by the quarry were too faded, and should have been renewed. Maybe it was his instinct for tying up loose ends, seeing things through, to avoid problems later. *Maybe it was that kiss.*

He let his eyes trail up, from her scuffed boots, over bare, dirt-streaked legs, to take in the way her denim shorts creased on the curve of her stomach, the way the cotton of her vest tugged tight across the bulge of her breasts. From the riot of her hair, she might have fallen out of a haystack. Probably had. So not his type, however lush her lips. However, she'd made his blood race.

Maybe he needed to keep Miss Awkward awake. Easier to keep from ogling her when she was conscious. He gave her a prod on the leg, and she blinked and sniffed, and turned to him woozily.

'So what do you do when you're not falling off horses?'

She hesitated, considered. 'This and that.'

'That's illuminating.' So why did he even want to know?

'I'm multi-faceted. Do lots of things.'

Like dodging the issue. 'Such as?' He wasn't backing down, and he sensed her get that. Sensed her caving in.

She shuffled her shoulders. 'Things like teaching dancing, exercising the pony, keeping an eye on my employer's Grandma, when the family's out of town. Except she's away now too. And I make collaged boxes, special ones, with lots of sticking and gluing. Satisfied?' She gave him a hard stare, as if she resented his intrusion. 'So what would you be up to if you weren't here? Slaving in the quarry?'

A counter inquisition? Only to be expected.

'Blowing things up. Big bangs and all that.' That pretty much covered it, he guessed. No need to say he headed up a worldwide mining and blasting company, with a mega-bucks turnover, and ran a fireworks subsidiary just for fun. Not that he left the board-room much these days. A desk-bound explosives expert, who'd lost his way.

Something about that reply shut her up, and she leaned back and closed her eyes again.

He sat back, scanned the busy waiting room, a world away from the smart, sparsely populated private clinics his family used. Beyond the silent TV with subtitles, an elderly man was helping his wife negotiate her walking frame past a couple exchanging grimaces over the heads of their squabbling kids. Next to them a couple of teenagers, seemingly joined at the hip, were clutching each other's hands, oblivious.

Now he'd started noticing, there were couples everywhere he looked. Damn Carrie and her coupledom flag waving. And they all seemed to be supporting each other. Supporting? Was that what couples did? The whole relationship thing was so far off his radar, he really wouldn't know. Not a place he planned on exploring any time soon. Probably not ever. He snorted loudly, at the thought of what he'd let himself in for with this darned dating challenge. He tried to rationalise the fact it was freaking him out. It had already caused him to wreck one car for chrissakes.

Realistically, it shouldn't bother him. He needed to chill, take it in his stride. But a month in, he still hadn't come across a suitable woman. He was a man who moved mountains, literally, on a daily basis. Jeez, what could be so difficult about a few dates? It was easy stuff. But he needed to tackle it, before he crashed any more cars. Okay, he had cars coming out of his ears, but not for wasting like that. But first he had to find a woman who was up to the task.

His eyes snagged on Millie again.

No. Absolutely not. Definitely not her.

Except she was objectionable enough to satisfy Carrie's criteria – a million miles from being compliant. And totally not what he'd ever go for in real life. A girl with riotous hair, and tattoos – one tattoo on her leg, he assumed there would be more – who majored

22

in sticking and gluing. He bit back a broad grin. Cassie would be gob-smacked and it would damn well serve her right. He already knew what fun it would be.

Shame then, it didn't seem right to go there.

Big shame, seeing as he'd pretty much racked up one date already, given they'd been here four hours. He couldn't think when he'd last spent that long with a woman. Women didn't particularly cross his path, other than at the wealth-dripping social occasions he attended, when he literally had to fight them off, and usually ended up taking his pick for a hot after-party liaison. It was all very well to talk about finding a suitable woman for the challenge as if women were ten a penny, but in his daily life they weren't. Women were pretty damned scarce in the working stratosphere he moved in, and suitable women were even scarcer. Where the heck was he going to find one? He couldn't fail the challenge before he'd even begun, because he couldn't find a woman.

'Sorry...' Millie had opened her eyes with a start and fixed him a grey-green gaze that sliced straight through his protective shell. 'But you don't smell like you work in a quarry.'

Hands in the air, he'd been over-zealous with the body spray this morning, and now she'd caught him out.

'A bit of a random comment for a Monday lunchtime. Where did that come from?' Not that he gave a damn, but more time to tailor his answer would come in handy.

Why was he still clinging to the pretence of being a quarry worker anyway? He could tell her something a whole lot closer to the truth without letting on to her that he was the CEO. But if he did that, he'd eliminate her from his challenge field at a stroke.

'Caught a waft/making conversation/passing time. You choose.' She threw him a smile he assumed was accidental. 'Anything rather than go insane with boredom.'

Something about that smile made him decide his answer. 'And

23

probably I don't smell of quarries because you caught me early on. By the end of the day it's a whole different story.'

So he hadn't ruled her out completely yet, according to the answer he'd given there. Not exactly a lie. Rather a judicious ambiguity. But she might not be available for his challenge, even if he ruled her in and that thought elicited a twang in his chest he couldn't explain. She didn't fit into his ideal, svelte-glossy-groomed-woman box, but that didn't mean there wouldn't be queues of other guys waiting to suck up her brand of curvaceous smolder. But if that was the case, why was she here with him? He watched as she drew one foot up onto the chair, and hugged her bent, bare leg close against one full breast, rested her chin on her knee, bit the fullest of lower lips, then closed her eyes again.

Pure sex kitten. Ready to play.

He shuffled in his seat, tried unsuccessfully to achieve some sort of negotiated settlement with his borrowed jeans, and opened Motor World. Not because he wanted to read about cars. He didn't. Cars were the last thing he wanted to read about. But Motor World was his only hope of keeping his eyes off the troubling body beside him.

***

'We've been here eight hours, and now you're telling me I can't go home?' Millie rounded on the nurse, her anger strangled by the panic that tightened around her throat. 'I won't stay here, I can't stay here...'

The last time she'd stayed in hospital... She gritted her teeth to banish that thought.

The nurse was insistent. 'You lost consciousness earlier, you have suspected concussion. For your own safety you need someone with you for the next twelve hours, otherwise we won't be able to discharge you.'

'Is there a problem?' Ed sauntered over, hands rammed into his pockets, his past-caring face long since worn out. All she needed. He'd been driving her crazy simply being here, all day long, with his superior expression, not to mention his shorter than short temper. Frankly, she'd met more mature two year olds. He obviously thought he was God's gift to someone; she just wasn't sure who yet. Sitting next to him had been like being rubbed all day with rough sand paper on bare skin. And he was going to love this. She already knew the way his disgustingly perfect features would twist as he gloated.

'They won't let me out unless there's someone to stay with me until morning.' She couldn't bring herself to say there was no-one she could think of to ask. Darned countryside, with hardly any people, her best friend off back-packing and after being here a year, no-one else she knew well enough to ask. All the family where she was living were away until the end of the week, even Grandma. It wouldn't have been like this if she'd stayed in the city. She had stacks of friends there. It was all very well being independent, coming to the country to get a free house whilst she built up her business, but there were times when it had serious drawbacks.

'My sister was ill for a long time, I can't stand medical environments.' She hurled that nugget at the nurse and the man, both staring at her, bemused. The truth, but missing out the real reason. Hopefully enough to explain her reluctance.

She tried not to remember how much she didn't want to stay here, how much she detested hospitals, how ill they made her feel after the last time. She threw one desperate glance in Ed's direction. 'Unless...'

'Unless what?'

'You wouldn't be able to..?' She screwed up every bit of courage and put her irritation of the day to one side. It was a measure of how desperate she was that she was even thinking of this, but, whoa, she was desperate. Desperate enough to force out a smile.

'Could you possibly stay with me for the next twelve hours?'

***

How the heck had it come to this? An hour later, pulling up outside Millie's cottage, Ed's internal panic alarm was blaring.

'I'll wait in the car while you go for your gear. Bring a quilt, my place is rough, I've got the builders in. And hurry up.' As if barking at her would improve the situation at all.

He had to be mad to be doing this, but somehow Millie had caught him off guard. Maybe it was the wild, haunted flare in her eyes. Stroppy woman and sex kitten had melted away, leaving one girl who was just plain scared, though perhaps the full-on curve of her lips in that one begging smile had swung it. Then his own instinct to work every situation to the max kicked in, and he was straight on the phone to Carrie, saying 'Dating Challenge on.'

When Millie re-appeared – not that he expected that to be any time soon – he'd drive into town, pick up a take-away, and then head back to the barn he was converting out on the estate. All agreed with Carrie as a suitable wealth-concealing, coupledom activity.

Twelve hours from now Date One would be over. All good.

Except now it came to it, he was the one bricking it, and he had no idea why.

CHAPTER THREE

MILLIE stretched out on Ed's threadbare sofa, loving the tea-lights placed at intervals around the floor edge, and the flickering shadows which danced up the rough stone walls.

'You okay there?' Ed leaned over the back of the sofa, and gave her quilt a tweak.

Was that a glimmer of a smile playing across his mouth, or just another ironic grimace? She'd definitely got her gratitude-goggles on here.

'Yep.' She nodded. Way more than okay in fact. Try couldn't be better. Perfect even.

Indian take-away, watching the sun go down on the terrace-to-be outside the huge barn doors, and washed down with alcohol-free beer, in case there was an emergency later. Bossy Ed had come through. So far, he was looking like a whole lot more than just a pretty face. And then all rounded off with luxury ice-cream. Now he was looking like a god. Not necessarily the best news for her, with her strict man-ban in place.

'The barn's still a work in progress, obviously. We've stripped out, done the roof and drains, and enough electrics to run a fridge. Should be good for a night of summer camping.' As he craned his neck scanning the roof timbers, she reeled as one glimpse of the exposed column of his throat fired a shiver down her back.

Then he sent her a grimace so close to a smile it made her tummy tumble into free-fall. 'Better than hospital, I guess.'

'You bet.' The secret cat-who-got-the-ice-cream grin she'd been guarding made a surprise escape, somehow plastering itself from ear to ear. Hopefully he'd turned away before he saw.

As for her man-ban, he'd given her no reason to think she had any chance with him. On the contrary, he was keeping his distance.

'So, if it's okay with you, I'll get on with that work I told you about.' He sauntered to the table by the doors, flopped onto a chair and opened his lap-top.

There you go. Point made. One more flip of her stomach as she took in those long legs, and the chiseled perfection of his cheekbones in the last of the daylight. Unusually, she didn't correct herself. For one night only, given she had a head injury, she would let her mental tongue hang out.

Now he'd lost the bad temper, if you overlooked his gloriously decorative side, there was something reassuringly basic and normal about this guy, sitting in his stripped out barn. It was going to be years before she had consolidated her independence enough to consider hooking up with anyone again, but when she did, she hoped it could be with someone like this. Someone hard working. Honest. As far away from trust-fund-on-a-plate Josh, and his rich-boy throw-away morals as she could get.

'Another beer? Hot chocolate? Ibuprofen?' Ed was at the fridge now, waggling a bottle. Smart black fridge too. She liked that. A bit like the one back home at her parents' place in London. Expensive, then. Good to see he'd got his chilled-beer priorities right.

'No thanks to all of those, I'm good.' Another escaping grin.

And thinking of home, she knew her family would blow a fuse when she chose to settle down with someone ordinary, so lucky it was a long way off then. Hopefully by that time she'd have proved she was capable of living without the intervention of their wealth, and was capable of making her own decisions, her own mistakes. She'd been independent of them for almost a year now, and although at times it had been tough, she knew that was how she had to play it. She had to be her own person.

'I've a lot to do here; I'll be busy for the next few hours at least.' He screwed the top off his beer as he walked back to the table and took a swig. Exposed his beautiful, kissable throat. Again. 'Settle down whenever you want. I'll leave the candles to burn. They should last beyond dawn.'

A shame he'd dismissed her so firmly. She'd have liked to know why a guy who appeared from the quarry in ripped jeans had so many hours of lap-top work to do. Costing out the building work perhaps? Too late to ask. She'd probably never find out now.

Pulling the quilt up under her chin, she felt a pang of disappointment that she'd dashed to sponge the blood out of her scalp, rush on some make-up, and pile up her hair, and he'd still shown no sign of noticing she existed. Not that she'd wanted him to. But as she closed her eyes to sleep, a tiny part of her was hoping she'd have the same dream as this morning. Okay, come clean. A large part. How ridiculous was that?

That when she woke up, it would be to find him giving her the second snog of her life.

***

Millie was woken at the crack of dawn, not by Ed snogging her socks off sadly, but by Ed shaking her shoulder, and bellowing in her ear.

'It's six thirty! The builders are on their way. I need to get you home.'

Less of the chocolate, more of the fog-horn voice this morning.

She groaned, dragged her fingers through her hair, and groaned again. 'Sorry – I'm not a daybreak person!'

'I gathered that already. Well done anyway. You've survived your twelve hours of surveillance, and now it's time to go!' He was sounding disgustingly awake, standing by the door, laptop in one hand, take-away rubbish and empties in a carrier in the other. 'Whenever you're ready...'

Twenty minutes later, she was unceremoniously ejected from the Land Rover outside her front door, and he'd driven off in a cloud of dust before she even had time to thank him.

***

There was definitely something to be said for a dawn start. By nine, Millie had caught up on most of what she'd missed yesterday, and was about to head for a shower when she heard the sound of hooves on gravel, and caught the un-mistakable neigh of Cracker the pony, on his way home.

Blast. She'd been hoping to make herself presentable, and then go up to the quarry to collect Cracker herself. Not that she wanted to attract the attention of anyone special, obviously, but simply to prove she wasn't always mud-streaked and bloodied, although seeing Cracker dragging Ed headlong into the yard more than made up for that disappointment.

'One mad pony and you're more than welcome to him after what he's just put me through.' Ed threw the reins at her, then delved into a pocket, and flipped out her missing phone. Same jeans, same shirt, same glorious body. But this time the thunderous brows lifted as his face split into a self-deprecating grin. He followed at a safe distance as she led the suddenly compliant pony towards his stable. 'Busy morning?'

She gave a 'whatever' shrug, tried to stop her head spinning from the heat of him. 'Sorted out a dance sequence for a private lesson this afternoon at the Country Club, though who knows why anyone would want to dance to Santa Baby, in July.' Accidentally-on-purpose forgetting to mention the 'B-for-burlesque' word. 'Packed up an order of my boxes to send to London, so now Cracker's home safely, I'll head out to the post office.'

His gaze honed in on her mucking-out shorts.

'After a shower, obviously.' *And she thought he hadn't noticed her!* How bad did she look? 'Thanks for last night, by the way. You saved my life twice yesterday.' She smiled, dipping as far behind her dangling hair as she could, as the thought of the snog made her cheeks whoosh scarlet. 'Anything I can do in return, just let me know.'

A last throwaway comment, meant politely, not needing a reply.

'You're welcome. All in a day's work for a Super-hero.' Inscrutable. No trace of embarrassment, at all. 'And there is something, something you can do, that is...'

'Yes?' She tilted her head, narrowed her eyes, her heart belting her chest wall as she waited.

'Come out with me tonight.' Just like that. Cool as a chilled beer. Unleashing a waterfall of shivers to cascade down her neck.

Oh lordy. 'You got me there, I'm sorry, I don't think so, I don't...'

Now he was the one narrowing his eyes, staring like she was gone out, planting his hands on his hips. Definitely not happy.

'Let's get this clear. I saved your life twice, and you're refusing me a date? Don't even think about it.' Chocolate voice like an incendiary now.

It was her turn to be chilled as a cool thing. Icey. Decided.

'I was planning to make you a thank-you batch of cookies.' She watched his expression slide from disbelieving to incredulous. 'I'm very sorry, but my life-plan doesn't include dates. I'm aiming for total independence.' Despite it being the truth, out loud it sounded ridiculous. But she couldn't be independent *and* have dates. Dates robbed you of your independence on every level.

'Excuse me? I'm talking about going out for an hour, not moving in!'

'Whatever.' She shrugged. This was not negotiable.

'Jeez, if you can dance around to Santa Baby all morning, you can damn well fit in an hour with me tonight.' Sounded pretty non-negotiable too.

But she'd got in first, and he knew that. Which was why he was backing away now, retreating. Heading out of the yard, his long legs swinging. Only as he got to the gate, did he turn his broad shoulders, and his even broader grin shone towards her like a beacon. He was laughing, she could see that now, and his dark voice bounced at her, off the gravel.

'Pick you up at seven.'

***

Rolling up at Millie's that evening five minutes early, Ed found the door open, so he knocked and went on in.

'Anyone here?' With a sweeping glance he took in a long room, open to the rafters, more like a gallery than a home. Passed a work table at one end, smothered in clippings, a sofa, and lots of lacey things in piles. Lots of stuff not in piles. 'Millie?'

He hoped she hadn't gone AWOL. Just his luck to hit on a date-phobic woman for this damned challenge. But having got one date under his belt, he wasn't going to give up that easily.

His gaze stopped abruptly at a multi-coloured line of satin corsets, hanging from a beam, laces dangling. Okay. Whatever. Plenty of people had corsets hanging in their living rooms. Didn't they?

And then he spied the pole – floor to ceiling, shiny chrome – and his face split into a grin the width of the sky.

Jeez. This had to be good. He'd calculated that tattoos and ragged hair would have maximum shock value for Cassie, but if Millie was a pole-dancer, that rated off the scale. Cassie really should have been more careful with her rules. Nice work. He'd landed on his feet here. Accidentally dating a stripper? Even if she was reluctant to date, from where he stood, this challenge suddenly couldn't get any better. Let the fun begin.

And then Millie appeared, eyes wide, startled to see that he was already here, but covering well, making his pulse surge way more than it should.

'Sorry I wasn't expecting you.'

Except she was, judging by her girlie pumps, and mini dress. Large black and white spots. He stifled a grin. *More jockey than race-horse, this one.* She turned, and he gave one mental thumbs-up as he clocked a patch of exposed, perfectly tanned back, that made him want to whistle, and a large bow, that put him in mind of a present waiting to be opened.

'Someone scrubs up well when they take their shorts off.' He shot her a wink.

'Ah, so wrong! I'd never go out without shorts.' She winked back and flicked up her voluminous skirt, to give a flash of the shorts below.

So that told him! Time to try another opening line.

'Nice place you've got here.'

'Great, isn't it? It isn't mine, I told you before, I get it in return for pony exercising, and Grandma-sitting. It lets me be...'

He cut in.

'Let me guess – independent? Why does that not surprise me? Sounds like a good deal, though having met the horse in question,

I'm not so sure. My shoulder's still in recovery after he dragged me down the road this morning.' He assessed the large open space again, this time being careful to avoid the pole area. Every surface was covered. 'I take it someone ransacked the place whilst you were away?'

He couldn't resist the jibe, if only to see how she came back at him, given the chaos.

'Artist at work.' She gave a sheepish shrug, apparently not offended. 'I prioritise, and housework comes last every time. Plus I hold on to anything I might use for my work. I'd have cleared up if I'd known the Tidy Police were coming.'

Nice return. One to raise the eyebrows. Neat was okay, but Tidy Police? If this was getting to know your date, he wasn't sure he liked it.

He'd made it to her work table now, and helped himself to a small patchwork box, by way of retaliation. 'So this is what you make?'

'Certainly is.' She shuffled, more uncomfortable with the scrutiny than she was letting on, he guessed. 'I specialise in collage – papering over the cracks.' She shot him a grin. 'At uni I did large scale pieces, but in terms of making a living it's more commercial to do smaller items, and people love boxes. I've hit on an unexpected niche-market, for original pieces. Every one's different.'

He nodded, examining the colourful surface, built up of cut and pasted images. 'I've seen something like it before. Can't remember where, though. I take it you sell them?'

'To exclusive stores in London mostly. That one is part of a French Theme series I'm working on. I'm building up, turning my art into business, filling in with the dance thing too.'

'Oh, the dancing.' *The dancing.* Slip this in, casually, drop it and let it bounce. 'So you're a lap-dancer? A stripper? Let me guess – to supplement your income?' He'd swung his head round, and was

34

eyeballing the pole, as her loud guffaw slapped him in the face.

'Typical man.' She was laughing now, those lovely lips drawing back to reveal beautiful, even teeth. 'You saw the pole, and assumed I'm a stripper? Sorry to disappoint you, but the pole's just a great way to keep fit. I'm no way athletic enough to be a professional.'

Damn. He squeezed the disappointment out of his voice. 'Not meaning to be nosey, but what's with the corsets then?'

'They're for the dancing. I teach Burlesque.'

'Ahhh, I see.' He didn't at all, but he wasn't about to admit it.

'Anyway, I thought you were taking me out? I haven't got all night.' She brushed back her hair, pushed a smile in his direction, presumably to sugar the impatience. 'So what are we doing?'

'A picnic!' He took a deep breath, unsure how she was going to take it, what with her date reluctance and all that.

Thank Cassie for this one. *No posh baskets and absolutely no champagne.*

'A picnic?' She chewed her thumb, and then fixed him with those deep grey eyes until he wished she would stop. 'That I can handle.'

***

'So why the date?'

Millie held up her glass of bubbly, and nailed him with her stare. It was only the way she chewed on what had to be the fullest lip in the history of pouts that gave any indication that maybe she wasn't as fearless as she made out.

This so wasn't going how he'd planned. Not that he had an exact plan.

The rug by the river, the cava and the smoked salmon had gone down okay. But she was so much more challenging than he'd anticipated, questioning everything, screwing answers out of him.

And she was jumpy as hell. No need for Cassie's rules about sex and first dates. At this rate he'd be lucky to have scored by the last one. *Memo to himself. More work needed in that department.*

'Why the date?' Repeating the question showed he didn't have a clue about the answer, and he didn't. Not any answer he could give her.

'Whatever the rights and wrongs, the blast caused your fall, and I wanted to make amends.' He replied, aiming for plausible.

'Aw, that's nice.' Her eyes crinkled into a smile, and she dipped a strawberry deep into the cream pot, and then bit into it. Showing off those delectable teeth. Again.

And that was it? Phew! An answer that wasn't another question.

'Yep, I'm really sorry about it.' And this wasn't faking, he really was.

'I don't think it was your fault.' Another easy response.

Under normal circumstances this was where he'd have made a move. Slid his hand over hers, looked deep into her eyes, said 'No hard feelings?' and got straight in there. Hell, by now he'd more than likely have been chasing that strawberry down her throat, his hand heading up her dress, and he wouldn't have found shorts up there either. But there was too much at stake here to move in too early and get blown off.

'So how come you can afford jeans like those, working in a quarry? Or have you hit gold?'

And she was off again. It was hard work keeping up with her. 'My sister's seriously loaded husband gave me a taste for good jeans with his cast offs, and great jeans are worth the investment. Now and again.' More ambiguity. He'd seriously underestimated how difficult he'd find the lying, and the whole pretence that he had no money. Darn careless of him to wear these particular jeans in the first place.

'Very cool, but I think I preferred the one's you wore yesterday.'

She spun him a wicked grin. 'I liked the rips.'

Predictably contrary. And how did she know the price of these jeans anyway, given how ultra-exclusive they were?

'These chocolate pots are scrummy, by the way. Where did you find them?'

Yet another question, fired as she sucked on a fingerful of dark chocolate mousse. Maybe Cassie had a point about him making bad choices with women. The Big Challenge. He'd ended up choosing a woman who couldn't be further from his ideal type, who not only refused point blank to date, but who was also a nightmare to handle. If he was going to have any chance of success here he was going to have to raise his game, massively.

Or he could give up on Millie, and begin again, choose someone easier, more polished, more suited to his tastes and needs. That was the obvious option, the easy option, the sensible option. But as he watched her kneeling now, all strawberry stained lips, tangled hair, and voluptuous curves, he knew wasn't going to give up. No way. Giving up was out of the question. He was going to raise his game, work out his strategy, and go for broke. Because the woman in front of him might be unsuitable, she might be crazy, reluctant, and jumpy; she could be everything he didn't want in a woman, but he couldn't give up on her yet – simply because he couldn't bear to let her go before he'd tasted her again.

***

At lunchtime next day, Millie arrived back from the Country Club to find Ed's Land Rover parked in the yard, and Ed sitting on her doorstep. Literally. Back against the door jamb, legs bent, jeans under a lot of pressure.

She grabbed a box from the car boot, and then walked towards him, blaming her suddenly feeble legs on the weight of the parcel.

'And where have you been?' As usual he was looking like a dream, as usual he was sounding indignant.

'A private lesson with my Santa Baby client.' She refused to ask him why he was here, and refused to let herself be pleased he was. 'At current rate of progress she will be ready to perform her Christmas Gift Dance for Christmas in eighteen months time, not six.'

'I've come to see how your head is, and ask if you've got any ketchup?'

She blinked. Sitting on her doorstep, *and* making random comments? 'Head still there, or it was last time I looked, thanks, and ketchup in the cupboard. Large bottle. Why?' Damn. Now she'd cracked, and asked.

'I've brought fish and chips for lunch.' He sprung to his feet, jumped towards the Land Rover, and returned with two packages and a grin that flipped her insides. 'You need a balanced diet to aid recovery. I'm taking responsibility.'

'Since when were fish and chips balanced?' She stifled a smile, went in and dropped the parcel on the already over-burdened sofa, then led the way through the house and out into the sun-splashed back courtyard, grabbing ketchup and cans of coke as they passed. 'They smell delicious, let's be wicked.'

She gave herself a hard kick for saying that, but he was already settling in at the outdoor table, rolling open the parcels of food. He pushed one towards her as she arrived.

'Pleased to see you're wearing your superior jeans today.' Saying that took her mind off his broad tanned hands, and the way the jeans in question sat so tantalisingly low and tight on his hips they made her stomach drop. All but took her appetite away.

'I'm not here to talk about jeans.' He picked up the ketchup, and put a neat blob by the side of his fish, then held the bottle out to her.

She took it from him, and squirted a winding trail all over her chips, clocking his disapproving frown. 'So? I like ketchup. It's a free world.' How could anyone be that judgmental about condiments? 'What *are* you here to talk about then?'

'You and this independence thing.' He paused, chip in mid air, and studied her gravely. 'I think you've got it all wrong.'

And who asked him anyway? She hated that shadowy hollows formed under his cheekbones when he looked at her like that, and the raw sensuality of his lips. The way his dark eyes melted. She scowled to cover that her insides were squelching again, and scraped at the angry prickles at the back of her neck.

'No, don't get cross, listen. No one's more independent than me, but you need to understand, being independent isn't about being alone. If you're hoping independence will make you stronger, you're wrong. What you have to realise, is that you can't be strong on your own, because humans aren't like that. People need each other. We get our strength by cooperating, by sharing talents, not from isolation.'

'And you are going where with this exactly?'

'Well, as I see it, your take on independence doesn't make you strong. Ultimately it makes you weak. And lonely too.' He was watching her carefully now, scrutinising her reactions.

Without thinking she dragged her hair back from her face, twisted it, and caught it on top of her head with a scrunchie from her wrist, so she could concentrate better. Her eyes locked on the lines of his mouth. Yesterday, at the picnic, she'd had a sudden, overwhelming sense he was going to kiss her, and all evening, her skin had been tingling, her treacherous body aching in anticipation. So wrong, so not what she wanted. But he was making her shiver again now, and once more she doubted her body's ulterior motives. No one as amazing as him would go for anyone like her.

Would they? 'Look, take me with my barn conversion. If I tried to do it on my own it wouldn't get done at all. I have the builders to help, and that makes it happen. The skill is to choose builders who are reliable.'

'And your point is?' Not meaning to be rude, but...

'That you'll only be truly strong and independent when you learn to accept help. You need people around you trust, who you can rely on.'

'Yeah, right.' *Been there, done that thanks.* With Rat-of-the-decade-Josh, who ran out the second she tried to lean on him. Her chest tight as a drum even as she thought about it now. She suppressed a shudder, but it took hold and leap-frogged down her spine.

'I'll give it some thought. Thanks for that.' *Not.*

She tried to sound firm enough to close the subject, and it worked. He went back to his lunch, eating with scary efficiency, and then rolled up the chip papers neatly as he finished, and stood up abruptly. 'Better be off then.'

Whatever. Millie stood up too, gave up all hope of ever getting where he was coming from, and followed him back towards the house. As he reached the doorway he paused, his large body barring her path, and grinned down at her. She hung on to her racing pulse rate, remembered to breath as his eyes, drilled into her.

'Don't suppose you'd give me a twirl on the pole?'

The guy was unbelievable. She shook her head, rapped out a good excuse, to hide her shock. 'After fish and chips? No way. If you wanted twirls you should have brought salad.'

He rubbed a thumb over his jaw, deep in thought. Narrowed his eyes. 'So twirls on the pole aren't hundred percent ruled out?'

What? Cheeky and persistent? And why the hell was she lapping it up?

'Get back to work before I kick your ass!' He'd dislodged himself from the doorway, got as far as the sofa, and stopped in front of the package she'd brought in earlier. 'So what's in the parcel then?'

She chewed her lip hard to cut her smile. He'd asked for this.

'If you must know, leopard-skin hand-cuffs, whips, long black gloves, under-bust corsets, over bust corsets, feather fans, suspender clips, and top hats. All times twenty.'

She was rewarded by his jaw on the floor, and his eyebrows on the ceiling.

'You are joking?'

'Nope.' She allowed herself a full-blown grin now. 'Supplies for a Hen Party I'm booked for – a Burlesque Workshop. Theme of Fifty Shades mean anything?'

He raised his eyebrows, gave a slow nod, and a knowing smirk, as he headed towards the door.

'I'll be back to tie you up later then.' His growl sent an avalanche of ice chips sliding down her back. 'I'll call in on my way home, to check you're okay. Maybe teach you more about this independence game. And don't forget, I'll be expecting that twirl!'

CHAPTER FOUR

LATER that afternoon, back in the sun-baked courtyard, working on her collages and her tan, Mille mulled over what Ed had said, as she concentrated on her French theme, and arranged a mix of roses, lace and tri-colours onto a box. Okay, the guy could lay on a scrummy picnic, and maybe fish and chips for lunch was a welcome change, but overall Ed was a complete pain in the butt, especially with the way he kept appearing. But he maybe had a point about fierce independence making you weaker, not stronger. It was good to hear a different viewpoint. She'd missed that since she moved here, yet another drawback of the isolation. It had become too easy to shut herself away, driving herself towards her goals. Maybe it was good to have some company, even if the company in question annoyed the hell out of her at times. Her life-plan was about taking responsibility for herself, her decisions, and her actions. Independence was what she'd become obsessed with as a means to achieve those aims, but what he'd said reminded her she needed to make sure she didn't lose sight of the bigger picture.

'Anyone home?'

Millie jumped as she heard Ed's voice reverberate through the house. What the heck was he doing rocking up in the middle of the afternoon, and her in her skimpiest bikini?

'I knocked, but you obviously didn't hear, so I let myself in.'

And then he was there, sauntering through from the house, talking to her, but not looking at her face. Eyes all over everywhere else. Devouring.

'Who finishes work at three thirty?'

Not that she wasn't completely at ease with her body – she was. Just not at ease with the way her skin sizzled under his scrutiny. She rubbed her nose with the back of a gluey hand, playing for time as she worked out her next move. Diving into the house to grab a vest would be preferable.

But how to get past him? He was leaning languidly across the doorway, all tanned brooding strength, eyes sootier than ever behind those amazing lashes, and uncannily silent. She saw his jaw clench imperceptibly, his broad shoulders shift.

A guy with a habit of getting stuck in doorways. Again.

'If you'll excuse me?' She took one firm step towards him.

He didn't move. Simply stared. And swallowed.

'Can I pass please?' She ignored the banging whack of her heart against her ribs, dragged her eyes away from the unmistakable blue shadow of an erection, forging against the denim of his jeans.

'Of course.' His eyes narrowed. Then he went sideways, back still grazing the wall, to make room, and his lips slid into the laziest of smiles. 'Any time.'

She hauled in a breath, hesitated, hardly trusting herself to pass him so close, hating that her body was betraying her, fizzing with excitement.

She needed to man up. What the heck was happening here? It was only one man, and one doorway she needed to get through. What could be so difficult?

Fixing her eyes firmly on the island unit in the kitchen, she set off.

Easy as. Except just after she'd made it past him, he snagged her. Not hard, not fiercely, hardly at all in fact, just the slightest graze of her forearm, then his fingers gently locking around her wrist.

Enough to make her heart-beat crash to a standstill, as her legs turned to hot syrup.

She stopped, turned a fraction, and the unbearable scent of him knocked her off her guard. As she rolled her eyes to meet his, she registered smoldering heat in their dark chocolate depths.

And the thought that any moment his mouth was going to come crashing down on hers.

'Millie..?' His voice was hoarse, gravelly.

Frozen as the goose-bumps raced up her arm, nipples like... 'What?'

He let her wrist drop, and he cleared his throat. 'I brought cakes. Any chance you could make some tea? '

And then there was nothing, except her hand, limp at her side.

As if she'd imagined it, as if it hadn't happened at all.

'Actually I'm just about to go out.' And then she was in the kitchen, grabbing a t-shirt from a kitchen stool and grappling her way into it.

A gut reaction. There was plenty of time for tea, so why was she pretending there wasn't? Lashing out because she was disappointed? Or saving herself from looking like a total fool when her over-active imagination made her think he wanted her? Hearing his voice advancing as he came in from the courtyard, she blurted out a hurried excuse.

'Sorry, I have classes this evening. I need to get ready. I should have said before.' She shrugged, diffidently. 'Some other time perhaps?'

'When are you back?' His eyes narrowed, more calculating now than smoldering.

Despite the blasts of hot air wafting from the courtyard, she shivered. 'Nine.'

Suddenly she wasn't sure she trusted herself to be around him any more. The more infuriating she found him in real life, the more she ached for a piece of him. She hated her body for playing tricks on her. No way could she be interested in any man right now, without de-railing her life-plan. She needed to get a grip on reality, she was a million miles away from ready for another guy. She had her priorities, and more to the point, she had her self-preservation instinct firmly in place. No guy, no matter how much animal magnetism he exuded, would be allowed to distract her and make her drop her guard.

'Catch you later then.' He was sauntering towards the door as airily as he had sauntered in. One cheery wave, one disgusting, tummy flipping, laid-back smile, and he was out of her hair. Easy peasy. But something about the set of his jaw made it sound like a threat not a promise.

***

Ed, batting down yet another country lane, grappled with the unwieldy steering wheel, and cursed as he bounced the Land Rover around yet another corner.

Basic transport. One wealth-concealing novelty I can do without, he thought. Same with the full-time countryside. Two more excellent reasons to dispatch this challenge, and fast. Kicking around the local quarries all day, relying on the phone and lap-top to keep tabs on the rest of the worldwide business, tracking the progress of the French firework extravaganza. He couldn't remember a time he'd been out of the office so long. Holidays weren't his thing, he was more a work kind of a guy. Good job his various teams ran like clockwork in his absence. Cassie was another reason to get the challenge over and done with. She was sitting with her high-and-mighty judge's hat firmly placed, ruling that casual cups of tea didn't count as dates, even if you did take cakes. Especially when you didn't have the tea, not that he'd actually admitted to that bit. Still, he mused, if this afternoon wouldn't have counted as a date in Cassie's darned book, then him being shown the door didn't count either.

No-one had ever refused him a date before. Ever. But Millie had, and she was rubbing his nose in it. And he was letting himself take it, all in pursuit of the challenge. Although maybe it would have panned out differently if he hadn't grabbed her. He was kicking himself for losing it like that, simply because she brushed by him practically naked.

Scraps of bikini, skin like hot toffee. Hardly worth the bother of dressing at all.

He wrenched the gear stick, crashing the gear-box to a howl as he missed the change.

He swore loudly.

He should be stronger than this. He knew he should be holding back, taking it slow, that if he didn't he risked stuffing up completely. So why the hell hadn't he?

And he hadn't even got the twirl on the pole she'd promised.

At least she'd conceded 'some other time' as she blew him off. The smallest chink in her defenses, but it hadn't gone un-noticed, and now he was here to capitalise on it.

Nine o' clock. Time to try harder, and this time he'd get it right. He was on his way to one more spontaneous, original, and low-spend date tonight, already run past Cassie, and this time he'd make sure it was a date that counted. Date 4. This time he wouldn't lose control. He'd give her all the space she needed, and work like crazy at making her feel comfortable. Hell, there were still so many dates left, there was plenty of opportunity to move things on later. Right now he needed to consolidate his position gently, and make sure she wasn't so jumpy that she wrecked his plan entirely.

He allowed himself a secret self-congratulatory smile as he flung the Land Rover into her drive, and let it spread to a triumphant grin, as he saw Millie, just home, killing her car lights, opening her car door, and pushing out one deliciously curvy leg.

Perfect timing.

Drawing up beside her now. Sensibly. Absolutely no skidding. Window down, and drumming his fingers on the battered side of the door. 'Hi! I thought I'd call by on my way home, just on the off-chance...'

'Home? I thought you didn't have a home.' And she'd already started, being exacting.

'I'm crashing with friends until the barn's ready.' He'd already started lying – besides, if he told her he had the run of the East Wing at his parents' Elizabethan castle, she wouldn't have believed him anyway. 'Coming for a spin? A warm summer's evening, the moon on its way up.'

Out of her car now, and eyeballing him across her car roof, she was dropping her eyes, hesitating, the way she did yesterday, when he talked about independence. He'd seen that same flicker of her eyelids when he got to the bit about relying on people, the flicker that told him she couldn't trust, wouldn't trust. With his own trust issues, he knew the signs. Except her problems would be way less screwed up than his, probably all down to some unreliable guy.

He shifted in his seat as his gut tightened. Trying to tempt her. 'Too nice to stay home.'

An inexplicable urge to flatten any guy who had hurt her surged through him, but his taut insides were more to do with the guilt about what ten dates could do to a vulnerable woman like her. The last thing *he* wanted to do was hurt her. There was no way he was in this for that. However fierce and independent she pretended to be, more than likely it was just a cover. Sometime soon he'd have to level with her, give her a clue what he was about, just so she knew.

He could feel her wavering.

He shot her a tenth of his emergency smile, not wanting to come on too strong. 'So what do you say then?' Leaned over, pushed open the passenger door, turned back and wound up the smile wattage. 'I promise you won't be disappointed.'

Two more aching minutes of deliberation, and he could feel her inward fighting, then suddenly it was over.

'Go on then.' And she was in, clambering up beside him, engulfing him with the heady scent of vanilla and hot skin, fighting to control the layers and layers of ragged net skirt, which still didn't hide her legs. 'And I'd better not be – disappointed, that is.'

Turning as he reversed, one glimpse of those bursting lips, so full of promise, through the tangle of her hair, reminded him to keep his eye firmly on the long term game. Strictly no rushing. 'I don't think anyone's going to be disappointed this evening.'

***

Keeping it light, banging through the gears, belting through the dusk on the family estate. As the balmy evening air buffeted their faces, Ed, yelled over the rattle and roar of the engine.

'You don't need to worry, I'm not here to de-rail your life.' He flashed her a grin that he hoped was honest, open, reassuring. 'I can teach you truck-loads about independence. It could be just what you need. My only promise is, I won't be staying.' He hoped that would be enough to cover it, for now.

'Great.' Millie returning his grin, hugging her knee, one tatty plimsoll heel wedged on the hard seat, as she shouted back. 'Thanks for that, I'll bear it in mind.'

A thrust of his pulse as he caught a flash of thigh through the ruffles, tangled with an inward groan of disapproval for her shoe on the seat. No way would she be sitting like that in one of his cars.

'Isn't this private land?' And she was onto him again.

He shrugged. 'Special dispensation – for quarry workers.' For this quarry worker, anyway, it was like playing in his own back garden, and he had a pang of disappointment that he couldn't tell Millie that. 'We're going to a great place, down by the river. I think you'll like it.'

If he was stuck with a damned four by four he might as well max it out. Veering off the track, he steered diagonally, bumping across the open field as he headed for the water.

'We used to come here to swim as kids.' Him, his five brothers and sisters, or rather the four of them still at home. That much he could tell her, that much at least was true. 'There's safe pool, where the river bends. Perfect on a summer's evening.'

They rolled to a stop under a tree, and as he cut the engine he could hear the rush of moving water.

'You're expecting me to swim?' Indignant didn't begin to cover it.

'It's not compulsory.'

'You should have said before, I'd have brought a swimsuit.'

'The one I saw you in this afternoon was hardly worth wearing.' That slipped out before he could stop it. 'But it's okay, it's private here, it's dusk, and there's no-one to see.'

'You're here.'

He mentally toasted her ability to ruin another evening, as he opened his door, jumped down, grabbed towels from the back, and flung her door wide. Needling, because she was denying him the enthusiasm the place deserved.

'For someone who makes a living taking your clothes off you're very prudish.' He joked.

There was enough light left in the day for him to know she

was looking daggers at him.

'I don't, and I'm not.' Add huffy and angry to awkward and exacting.

He had to dig deep, and make a big effort to pull her around. Somewhere, in the dusk, amongst the ruffles of her skirt he found her hand. Warm. Slender. Surprisingly small, given the flock of butterflies it released in his chest. Closing his fist around it, he squeezed. 'Just come for a walk then.'

He felt her give in, her hand flexing away from his grasp. And she was out, taking off, slipping ahead of him through the shadows, and by the time he reached the water's edge she'd already kicked off her shoes and was ankle deep, ruffling her skirts, stamping.

'It's freezing!'

Despite the chill, he sensed her thawing.

'That's the whole point. It's invigorating, but it's easier if you do it a lot because your skin gets used to the cold.'

She was in up to her knees now, skirt bunched up, tucked under her short denim jacket. Standing still, as the moon slid up the sky, and emerged over the tree tops on the opposite bank.

'Look, Ed.' Her voice was urgent, and she was pointing upstream. 'The moon's lighting up the water.'

'I told you you'd like it. And moonlight swimming is something else.' He hesitated, not knowing whether to push it. 'You don't have to do it, but I'm going in.'

He flung down the towels, shrugged off his shirt, whipped down his jeans, and two seconds later he let out a shout as he stormed in, and the icy water hit his skin and smacked the breath from his body.

***

Buff naked man alert!

And even if it was almost dark, what a body!

The deep breath Millie drew as she saw Ed hit the water went on forever, but still didn't seem to be giving her enough oxygen. She shook her head, raised an eyebrow in the shadows, and smiled silently, as she watched him gasping at the chill, his head bobbing as he jack-knifed in the silvery water.

'Careful you don't drown, I don't have a lifeguard certificate!' she called, shouting anything to cover her confusion.

And that had pretty much sealed it. She was going to have to go in too. There was no way on earth she could stand here and watch him emerge from the water. It had been bad enough sitting next to him in the Land Rover, watching his lean tanned forearms wrestling with the steering wheel. The sight of him naked would push her already surging hormones beyond the danger zone and out the other side.

Back there, the thought of swimming with him had set her alarm systems jangling, until he'd found her hand. That couldn't have made her move faster if he'd been electrically charged. But going phwoaaarrr at the sight of a hunky male was one thing. Acting on it was something else entirely. One strict no-go area. Or it was when she had her rational head on. Despite the warmth of the air she shivered again, chewing her nail as she struggled to work out the ambiguity of her reactions. Traveling along those bumpy rutted lanes seemed to have knocked the sense clean out of her.

'If you're coming in, fast is the only way to do it!' He was thrashing around, still facing the bank. 'That way you don't feel the cold!'

Thanks for that Mr Mitchum. She damn well would be fast, not because of the cold, but because she had to take him by surprise. But what to wear? She weighed up the options. Shorts and vest? Knickers and bra? None of the above?

51

Playing for time. 'What's it like in there?'

'Cool!'

Were those his teeth chattering? Just do it. Hadn't he just told her back there he wasn't going to be sticking around? So she had very little to lose. *So much to gain.*

Three seconds, she was down to her underwear, one more and she was slicing through the water, her whole body shrieking with shock.

'Watch out banshee, don't put your head under, or you'll mess up your cut!' He was laughing at her now, lunging towards her, splashing exuberantly. 'Good or what?'

She was wading, water up to her shoulders, laughing, shivering, juddering, gasping, not caring that he was in front of her now, gathering the strands of her hair that were dripping round her shoulders, and bunching them around the back of her neck.

'Chilly.' Her teeth rattled as she slid to a halt. 'Like you said.'

She shuddered, wildly. Nothing to do with the cold. Knowing she should back away, splash away, run away, anything to put distance between her and this man who was tipping her force field upside down, his mega attraction dragging her to him, when she knew she should be running for the hills. And her limbs refusing to make any movements at all as she drank in his sculpted cheekbones, glossed with moonshine, that sexy sardonic twist of his lips, those damp locks of hair dangling over his forehead.

Now he was smiling, and her stomach was doing somersaults. Reaching out, she put one quaking hand on his upper arm to steady herself. Her touch met with his deliciously slippery skin, and the flex of deep muscle. The other hand went on his shoulder, then slid along, around, slithering onto his back, catching the shudders reverberating up his spine in her fingers, as her heart banged crazily against her ribs. Holding her breath, she pushed her hand into the wet tangle of his hair, and the undulations of his skull were firm and real under her finger tips. She knew that this time it wasn't a dream, because his breaths were hot and ragged on her cheekbone.

Reaching up, grazing her mouth along the stubble, she found the edge of his bottom lip, feathering with her tongue, teasing, asking, demanding. And all the time, he was still, remote, stony, standing like a shivering statue.

She shifted, jerked as the length of his erection banged against her pelvis.

'Sorry.' One mumbled apology

'Don't be.' His growl was feral. 'I'm not.'

Then his mouth slid over hers and she dived deep into the tangling, demanding vortex of his kiss. Hungry. Starving. Longing for the taste, pushing her breasts against the rock of his chest, sliding her calf around the sinews of his thigh, reveling in the raw heat of his mouth.

This was real. The gruff moan in his throat as she tugged on his hair was real, the pressure of his hands on her waist as he lifted her was real.. Buoyed by the water, she wrapped her legs tight around his waist, locked her arms around those rippling shoulders. And boy, the volcano of desire, pounding between her legs was real, as she moved against his pelvis. Letting her eyes slide upwards to check the moon was still there, finding it blurred by the aching need in her body.

Then, she suddenly found that she could breathe again.

And she was rocking, gently, moving against him as he was striding towards the bank, the air cold on her emerging skin.

And then he was disentangling her, unwrapping her legs, unhooking her arms, and as her dangling feet hit the mud of the shore, he bent, flipped her a towel, and she knew it was over.

CHAPTER FIVE

MILLIE always got up extra early on Thursdays. With no classes to distract her, she liked to exercise Cracker at day-break, then hammer on with her box making. But this morning she was doing more thinking than gluing, and more cursing than thinking. And if that wasn't enough, she was running short of material for her French-themed line. She'd severely under-estimated how much she was going to need.

Another tri-colour bit the dust, as she slammed her fist into the table. She growled, and a half-finished box flipped across the surface, toppled off the edge, and skidded across the tiled floor. 'Marie-frigging-Antoinette!'

'See you tomorrow.' That's what Ed had shouted after her as he'd shot off in a spray of gravel last night. 'See you tomorrow.'

Just the thought of it made her furious. She'd put herself out there, taken a risk, totally against her better judgment, and he'd thrown it back in her face. All her fault. She should have kept a grip of herself, not jumped him like some sex-starved harpy, not assumed that just because for an instant she'd had an inexplicable urge to eat him whole, it was reciprocated. It had been utterly humiliating, being carried from the water like a kid, but it served her damn well right for deviating so far from her plan. Last night had been one bad, bad call. Her life-plan was there for a reason, and she should darn well stick to it.

See you tomorrow? She snorted disgustedly. How about – not if I see you first mate?!

And just to prove she meant business, she'd put on her scrattiest playsuit, and left her hair unbrushed.

Not that she was expecting callers.

She heard the knock first, then the clunk of the door handle. Then the rasp of his voice sent her heartbeat into overdrive.

'Anyone home?'

This far through the day and no contingency plan for if he walked in. She really *wasn't* functioning properly.

He sidled in, looking as if he'd just stepped out of a Vogue ad. 'I've brought salad. Thought you might like to give me that twirl.'

And her legs turned to jelly, though this time she was the one growling.

'You'll be lucky!'

Noticing the fallen box on its side on the floor, he stooped to pick it up, turning it nonchalantly between his fingers.

This one already had her ABB signature stuck firmly in place.

No way was she up for questions about her Amelia Brunswick Brown alter ego, the moneyed parents, the running away. She'd made the hardest decision of her life when she was Amelia. Not that she'd ever forget that. She lived with the burden of it every day. But she'd made her new start as her abbreviated-alias, Millie Brown, and it was imperative she kept Amelia hidden.

'I'll take that, thanks!' She snatched it, and spun it back onto the work table before he had time to blink.

One grin turned to grimace, a roll of his still-too-dark eyes, then moving on to the kitchen, he plonked down a carrier from the deli in town, and a pretty glass bottle of something fizzy. 'Have you eaten today?'

She desperately scraped her fingers through her hair, regretting the playsuit choice now. 'Nope.'

He sniffed his disapproval, pushed one delectable dark wave off his forehead. 'It's bad to skip breakfast, even if you have just got up.'

She was open-mouthed, reeling at the onslaught, knees weakening, despite her best life-plan resolutions. 'I've been up since five, if you must know.'

Now he was the one with the surprised face, already settled in though, back against the work surface, legs crossed, arms folded, as if yesterday never happened.

'Jeez, you must be starving! Grab some plates then, and we can dive straight in.'

***

'Have you got grated carrot?' He pushed the plastic container across the table towards Millie, as if vegetables were going to make anything better. If he had wondered how that delicious pout would look when she seriously wasn't happy, now he knew, in spades. Even worse than at the hospital.

He'd counted on difficult, not impossible. So, how to rescue the situation once you'd blown a girl off, even if it was for the best of reasons? If he hadn't pulled out of that kiss when he did, he'd have been inside her within a minute.

'Olives and tomato?'

She nodded. Took it in silence.

'Dressing?' Ditto.

The trouble was that last night she'd spun him so far out of control that the only thing he'd known to do was stop. He cleared his throat.

'Last night, in the water...' He had her full attention immediately, and withered slightly under her grey-eyed glare. 'I didn't want to stop...'

'So why did you?'

Reproachful. One step easier than accusing.

'It was going too fast. There was too much heat. You must have felt it?'

'Maybe...' Relenting. A touch.

'I needed to be sure you wanted...' Not quite right. He cleared his throat. 'I needed to make sure our aims coincided – before we went any further.'

The tiniest twitch of a secret smile. 'And?'

'I told you before, I'm a short term guy, I don't do commitment.'

'Huh...' One snort. Of recognition?

'The way I work, there's no obligation, and no disappointment. No emotion, no broken hearts, no-one's let down.' He baulked inwardly at this impromptu mission statement, polished like he paraded it on a regular basis. 'It's a win win situation.'

'Ah.' She nodded slowly. Narrowed her eyes. 'You mean a kind of friends with benefits thing?'

He hesitated. Big time.

She really didn't get this, did she? Since when had he felt the need to explain himself to a woman about sex anyway? And since when did yesterday's mascara smudges look so sexy?

'Less of the friends, more of the benefits I'd say, majoring on the pleasure.' And so much tidier than saying 'sex for the hell of it'.

He caught her tell-tale eyebrows as they flew skywards. This had to be a whole new ball-game for her.

'Thanks for explaining. I'll give it some thought.' Gently chewing on Parma ham, lips curving into a smile, but for herself, not for him. Eyeballing him straight now, as she fiddled with one slender, slipping shoulder strap. 'Like I told you before, I don't really have space in my life for guys right now, however they're packaged. Put last night down to the water and the moonlight, it was an

57

aberration, and I promise it won't be happening again.'

Great. She was talking, even if she was back to the no-guy track.

As if anyone who'd had her legs locked around them would believe that.

'More asparagus?' His eyes had snagged on her shoulder. Bare. Lightly freckled. And what was she wearing? Definitely no corsets today, no underwear at all, judging by the speed of his pulse, the just-got-up look acting like a come-to-bed look.

'Are you still in your pyjamas?'

She held an olive between her fingers, gave him mouth-watering glimpses of her tongue and perfect teeth, as she stripped the flesh off the stone before she deigned to reply. 'Nope, this is day-wear. A one piece shorts playsuit, elasticated at the waist, the perfect combination of comfort and practicality.' She flashed him her first full-on grin of the day. 'The rabbits are ironic, by the way.'

'Rabbits?' Who the hell said anything about rabbits?

'Yellow and green ones, in the print, see?'

As she leaned forwards to show him, he missed the rabbits, caught the glorious thrust of bare breast through the fine creased cotton, and was fiercely reminded how tight jeans and erections didn't mix, especially not on bar stools. Casually, he slid to stand, to ease the problem.

'So, if we're done with the salad shall we progress to the pole?'

Sauntering across, coming to rest with his shoulder against the wall. Possibly a rash move, given the constriction difficulties he already had, but it was a distraction. Not that he thought there was the remotest possibility she was going to oblige, but somewhere along the line getting a spin from her had become a challenge, and he knew how he was with challenges.

'Okay. You win.' She was coming towards him now, all self-contained, self-assured.

All in control.

And then he was picking his jaw off the floor. First at the way she caved, then at the way she rose high onto her tip-toes, stretched out one easy arm, grasped the pole, followed with a bend of her knee, a twist of her ankle, and then swung, elegantly, arching, oh-so-slowly. Spinning, one, two, three mind-blowing revolutions, before she pushed gently back to standing again. Easy as, and sexy as hell, even though there was nothing overtly sexual about it.

One compliment, reverberated low in his throat. 'I like it.'

'Me too.' She shuffled her shoulders, shifted her feet, stood back. 'it's fun, it's great for fitness. And it's empowering.'

Too true. Certainly gave her power over him. Hell, right now he'd have done anything she asked. Because there she was, all rough and unkempt, so different from his usual type, yet somehow the dizzying haze of sexuality she exuded, was knocking him off balance

'So what about the lap-dancing that's not lap dancing? Will you show me that too?'

All mixed up with an un-nerving dose of vulnerability. That had to be was what was throwing him.

'The Burlesque? You think it's about sleaze, don't you?' And she was back to accusing. 'What you said yesterday about me making a living by taking my clothes off?' Facing him square now, she rolled her eyes, shook her head, and gave another of those huffy sighs he was becoming so familiar with.

'And it's not?' Eyeing the corset tossed lightly on the sofa, and mentally pouring her into it.

'Burlesque is different. It's always been about entertainment, and glamour, and aesthetics, not just about striptease. The stars of the thirties were independent, successful women, who dreamed up amazingly innovative performances. Today's Burlesque is a modern take on that, it's about women celebrating who they are, rather than conforming to stereotypical ideas of beauty. You don't have to be a tall, skinny model to succeed – it's more about expressing individuality. Every dancer has her own special thing.'

'So do you perform in public?' The thought sent an unexpected snake of prickles down his spine, and not in a good way. His throat constricted, and it seemed like forever as he held his breath, waited for her reply.

'It has been known, but not any more. And never all the way.'

'And you had a thing?'

'Mine was cream. It began as a joke, and kind of caught on, but I'm not in the performance league. I joined the Burlesque Club in Freshers' Week at Uni, and it went from there. All I do is spread the word, have fun, and ultimately make women feel better about themselves. Whether its classes, or Hen Parties, I teach women the moves, give them a taste of the glamour, and show them how to express themselves so they can feel attractive. Feeling desirable is very empowering for a woman.'

Panic over. He was breathing again. 'I don't doubt it.'

Though quite why he was panicking was beyond him.

She shrugged. 'Times have changed. Women these days don't wear high heels because they want to please men, they wear them because they want to please themselves. Women who are powerful in their everyday lives can take one step more, and have that bit of extra sensual power over men. Or they may choose not to bother, of course.'

Like she had.

Except she had been bothered enough to kiss him. Twice. Two explosive kisses that made him dive in to capitalise on the women in control line..

'If you are serious about being truly independent, you really need to perfect the art of no-strings sex. That you *would* find empowering, and fun.' He commented, waiting to see where it got him.

'Really...' Biting her lip, suppressing a smile. Was she mocking him here? 'Like you were suggesting earlier?'

'I'd promise to be temporary, and something tells me there's lots of heat to burn.'

Gently suggestive. Paving the way, hoping for a shift.

'Thanks for the offer. I'll get back to you if I decide I'm interested. Don't hold your breath though.' She watched him, coolly detached now, as he moved back to the kitchen, neatly stacked the remains of lunch in the fridge. 'Did you bring dessert?'

Always leave them wanting more.

Except she didn't. Apparently.

'Dessert's later. I'll pick you up at seven.'

And for the first time he was sensing that the way forward may not be as simple as he'd planned.

***

'So what kind of a dessert girl are you? Let me guess?'

They were in a wine bar in town, the sort with artfully mismatched chairs, a chalk-board on the wall, and a clientele who looked effortlessly perfect, even though Millie suspected they'd spent a long time getting that way.

Ed wagged the desert menu at Millie, and narrowed his eyes in a way she wished he wouldn't, simply for the sake of her rapidly descending stomach.

'You definitely won't choose sticky toffee pudding, and something tells me it won't be the crumble and custard either, even though it is rhubarb.'

Yet again, she'd relented, caved, and here she was, melting under his gaze, hanging onto every chocolatey syllable, with her heart squishing as she noticed his broad tanned fingers slipping on the back of the menu card. *Glory, she could fall here.* But she was damned determined she wasn't going to.

'And I know it won't be the sundae, even though whipped cream might have been your thing.' He tapped his thumb nail on his almost perfect teeth. 'I'd have asked you for a full meal, but I knew you wouldn't come. Your hair looks nice up, by the way.'

Blushing at his compliment was not the best idea either, especially when she'd put in such an effort to look sophisticated, to counteract him catching her in her playsuit earlier. And damn, for how well he read her, after knowing her such a short time. Disgustingly perceptive. No way would she be here if he'd asked her to commit to more than dessert.

'Got it!' His eyes crinkled into a triumphant grin, as he tossed the card on the table. 'You'll go for the crème brûlée!'

'Always do.' She spun him her lightest smile. 'My grandmother is French.' As if that explained anything. At least it filled the acres of silence left by her shock at his accuracy. She picked up the menu, screwing her face up as she pondered. 'I'm going to guess you'll have the ginger tart, to match your eyes.'

Had she just said that? About his eyes? Double damn.

'Didn't know you'd noticed, but as it happens I will go with the ginger. I'll order now.'

Millie watched him sidle up to the bar, took a second to admire the muscular thrust of his butt in his pale grey chinos, then watched the barmaid swoon ever so slightly as she took his order. Not her fault. That was how Ed Mitchum affected women.

And she, Millie Brown was personally turning him down. Flat.

One day, down the line, she'd be proud of herself for this.

And then he was back, with his non-stop interrogation. 'French grandmother, eh? So what about the rest of your family?'

Nice diversion, even if she didn't discuss her family, especially not with him.

'Parents, two sisters, I'd see them more if I wasn't so busy.'
Pointless telling him she was a rebel middle child, how she couldn't
stay in touch because she couldn't bear to see her sister. Nor any
need to give him any inkling of the trouble she'd caused, how she
didn't want to see them, how hard she was trying to do things
on her own.

'More of your independence, huh? Talking of which, have you
thought any more about my too-good-to-miss no-strings offer?'

So he'd picked it up anyway, and turned it straight around, taken
it somewhere even more uncomfortable. Nice one, Ed.

'No, and no.' And lying on both counts, given that she'd hardly
stopped thinking of no-strings sex with him, even if she wasn't
going to take him up on it. Not even with the promise of it being
temporary, with a fast finish.

'That's a shame. Still, your loss.'

And his grin the width of the wine bar, to show, she guessed,
that he didn't give a fig.

And then their desserts arrived, and she had to bear watching
him carefully pouring a smooth stream of cream onto his plate.
Then, try to peel her eyes away from the hollow at the base his
neck, as he negotiated his way into his ginger tart.

'Not eating?'

'Sorry, I was just thinking.' Swooning like a barmaid, more like.

One divine sliver of crème brûlée slithered off her spoon and
down her throat, as she began to eat.

'I've been thinking too.' He rested his spoon on his plate. 'I
have to go away for work.'

'Oh?'

One word. Desperately trying not to let her dismay crack into
her voice.

Why the hell did that make her feel so bad? Just because he'd
pestered her all damned week, supposedly to get her used to being

with people again, she shouldn't mind him going away.

'France. Provence. To do a firework display.'

'You do fireworks?'

Fighting the ridiculous hollow feeling in her gut, she rammed a massive spoonful of crème brûlée into her mouth.

'I do explosives, I major in big bangs of any sort, fireworks included. If I can wrangle you an air ticket, on the company that is, I thought you might come too?'

Millie's gulp of surprise took her crème brûlée straight down her windpipe. She gasped and spluttered, rasping for breath as she choked. Loud and long and horribly hard.

By the time Ed had banged her thoroughly on the back, and the swooning barmaid, now swooning even more drastically, had brought her an emergency glass of water, Millie knew she had to be scarlet.

Panting. Dying of embarrassment. Puce to her earlobes.

Not attractive.

Excuse me. Had he just asked her to go to Provence with him?

'No strings.' He flashed her a grin which morphed into a grimace as he realised his gaff. Jumped in hurriedly to make it clear. 'No strings, not as in no-strings sex, just as in come anyway? With or without benefits?'

Provence, with Ed? That would be melting, mocking, heart-stopping Ed?

No way. Out of the question.

Absolutely, definitely, completely, undeniably, irreconcilably not.

'I thought it might be good for your French box things? You could pick up more material?'

Good point. From a box point of view, a trip to stock up on memorabilia to cut up and paste would save her bacon, but life wasn't just about boxes. Ed was the last man in the world she should go to Provence with, boxes or no boxes, because Ed in Provence would be too tempting. And she did have her commitments – lessons to take, ponies to look after. Except the family were back now to look after Grandma and Cracker, and her private lesson calendar was practically empty due to the holiday season. But it was way too dangerous, tantamount to life-plan suicide.

'Thanks.' She heard her voice, far in the distance, but wasn't aware she was speaking the words. 'That would be amazing. I'd love to come.'

Had she truly just said that?

What *had* she let herself in for?

CHAPTER SIX

'SO how was your Fifty Shades weekend?'

One week later, fresh from picking Millie up from the airport, they were howling along the lanes of Provence in the economy rental car Cassie had sanctioned. Thanks to the fiercely negotiated pay-off for the luxury of the free flight, they were heading towards a tent. Ed wasn't sure what Cassie expected him to pull out of the bag for a low-budget weekend away, but judging from her strict terms, it certainly hadn't been this. He got the feeling she thought he was pushing his luck, that taking Millie this close to the family chateau was sure to blow his cover. But he was confident that Millie would have no reason to suspect the truth. He would be there, as he was every August for this event, working alongside the guys on the firework team, setting up the biggest pyrotechnic display of the summer in the region, and he planned to keep her at a distance from both his the team and the family. It was his one hands-on gig of the year these days, before he climbed back into his suit. Considering that the whole village would be heaving with visitors, and in the throes of the Summer Festival, he couldn't see there would be a problem. Not as long as there weren't any storms. And as far as storms went, he had everything crossed, tightly. As Cassie had said, she didn't give much for his chances if he had to take refuge in the Chateau, but then torrential rain in August was not that common.

'The Fifty Shades gig was awesome, thanks.' Millie, smiled radiantly at him, and blew all thoughts of rain from his mind. 'The whole weekend went down really well. We managed to release the hunky bouncer the bride handcuffed herself to, and the head bridesmaid wasn't supposed to show off her pasties on the dancefloor, but otherwise it was all good.'

'Pasties?'

'Stick on nipple covers. All the guests were given a pair, as part of the package, except they weren't meant to be worn out. These ones had rhinestones, and pink tassels, and I'm sure the clubbers of Nottingham appreciated them.'

Ed felt his eyes widen, as he caught a flash of her wicked smile. If she was winding him up it was working. Big time.

Since he arrived here alone five days ago, he'd plagued himself, going over and over what had made him ask her to come to join him. He'd expended mega amounts of energy, pretending to Cassie that it been a pre-meditated part of his challenge strategy, but he knew that was all bull. Because one glimpse of the vulnerable curve of Millie's neck in the wine bar last week, the big bang from that kiss in the water still reverberating round his head, and the invitation had come tumbling out, in one uncontrolled, spontaneous, ill-considered gush. In the end he'd rationalised it as his honed instinct for milking every chance to the max. But, no denying, it had shaken him. So having succumbed to one non-strategic impulse in the wine bar, it became doubly important to perfect his approach for the remainder of the challenge.

He'd known from day one that Millie was jumpy. It hadn't taken a brain-surgeon to work that one out. All his talk of no-strings sex was wishful thinking, completely inappropriate for anyone as fragile as her. For that, on reflection, was what he'd decided she was. Fragile and fearful.

Damage limitation was the name of the game now. If she took fright and fled she'd send the whole darned operation down the pan. He'd reached Date 7 of a ten part challenge here, and the closer to the end he got, the more there was at stake, and the more careful he needed to be. He needed low risk here, and the low risk strategy now was to back right off, and make sure there was no physical contact before their last date, whatever the temptation. That was the only way to be sure he'd nurse her through to the end.

But if that last sizzling smile was anything to go by, he was in for a hard time.

Millie appeared to have come off the plane with a whole load more sass, as if she'd left a hefty slice of reticence back home. He braced himself for one long weekend of temptation, which he would definitely be resisting, because given the size of her travel bag, she couldn't possibly have brought much more with her than nipple tassels.

He inclined his head towards her bag in the back seat. 'You're traveling light.'

'Yep, always do. It's easier in economy if you only have hand baggage, though you'd be surprised how many floaty dresses one determined packer can fit in a case like that.'

And for a minute there she sounded like she knew another side of travel.

He gave a throaty guffaw. 'Usually on a private jet are we?'

She didn't reply, but the unexpected pink flush he caught invading her cheeks as she turned her head away from him made him uneasy. But only for an instant.

'So, you're okay with camping? I've juggled the budget. What I saved on my hotel went towards your flight.' Feeling the need, for Cassie's sake, to make it clear. 'Special dispensation for the Chief Firework Organiser, we get to pitch the tent in the grounds of the village Chateau.'

'That's cool! Camping's good, and it kind of goes with the sort of guy you are.'

'Meaning?'

'Half-built barns, picnics, river swimming. They're all down-to-earth, no frills; a bit like you, with your ripped jeans and your beaten-up Land Rover. But that makes them more real, more fun, somehow.'

On track with the deception then. His lips twitched into a grin. 'We aim to please.'

'When my sister was ill, it was the simple things we got the most out of. Fireworks are like that too I guess. Basically only bangs and bright flashes, but they give a huge thrill. They suit you.' She spun him a smile, pushed her fingers into the wind-swept haze of hair, then tucked the heel of her battered cowboy boot on the car seat, and hugged her knee to her chest.

Feet on seats? Again?

And one more Cinderella dress. If it hadn't been for the way the layers of ragged skirts fell away to reveal a satisfying stretch of tanned thigh, he'd have had to admonish her for the foot thing. And whoever would choose to wear calf-high boots in a Provencal summer?

'With any luck we'll manage more than a few bangs and flashes.' He grinned ruefully. 'What was wrong with your sister?'

'A rare sort of leukemia. For years we didn't think she'd pull through, but she's all good now, started a family and everything.' She chewed hard on her thumb nail, as a shadow flickered across her face.

Damn, he hadn't meant to upset her. Hadn't she implied her sister was better? He was certainly right about her being all over the place.

Weaving a gauzy section of skirt tightly round her fingers, she sent him a too-bright smile he saw right through. 'How come you

69

got into blowing things up anyway?'

A question he'd usually have dodged, but suddenly it was a relief to have something to tell the truth about. 'Blake from the quarry came to my rescue when I was a kicking teenager, and harnessed my self-destructive tendencies. Put them to better use, blasting rock faces. Turned me on to big bangs, and I was hooked for life.' Not mattering that it was more than he'd willingly revealed to anyone before.

'And what exactly were you kicking?'

And so like her not to leave it at that.

'Family trouble. I was rebelling. Against the whole over-bearing parent thing.' The truth again, but this time artfully shrouded, missing out the whole odd-one-out-in-the-family mess of the matter. Protecting himself.

One murmured acknowledgement, then she cleared her throat. 'And are the preparations for your display going well?'

He tapped his fingers on the steering wheel, and moved on quickly 'We're getting there. It may just be a small French village, but they take their summer fireworks very seriously, so it's actually a big job.' Which dovetailed perfectly into talking about plans for the morning. 'I'll be tied up with it most of tomorrow, but I can drop you in Avignon for the day. There's a vintage market where you should find great pickings for your boxes.' And keeping her at a convenient distance, would give him a double advantage. Not only would it stop her uncovering his family's assets, it would also make his hands off policy a whole lot easier to stick to. Whatever Cassie thought, he was confident he could pull this off.

'Brilliant! Sounds amazing!' she beamed at him.

He rubbed a thumb across his jaw, wishing her grateful smile didn't knot his stomach with guilt for the way he was using her. As the baking patchwork of olive groves and peach orchards and vineyards flashed by, he drummed his fingers on the steering wheel some more, and tried to figure out what the hell was going on. Because when she'd wandered out into the arrivals hall at the airport, with her scuffed boots and her dress in shreds, for one awful moment he'd had an irrational, almost uncontrollable urge, to sweep her into his arms.

Ed Mitchum. Uncontrollable? Irrational?

No way. He needed to get a grip. All he was doing here was moving the challenge along nicely. That had to explain why he was happy see her. All week he hadn't been certain she'd even show, and now here they were, getting the whole awkward weekend-away thing over and done with. Relief didn't begin to cover it. There was no way, after the effort he'd put in this far, that he was going to be forced to repeat the whole dratted process again with some other woman. He was sure if he handled the situation right, he'd be home and dry in no time, Challenge in the bag. Maybe not quite what he'd had in mind the moment when he blurted out the invitation. But if that's what it was going to take, he was happy to go along with it. And the more he thought about it the more sure he became.

The game he played this weekend was going to be strictly hands-off.

***

Millie caught her breath as she saw the clustered buildings of the approaching village rising from the landscape of lavender fields.

'I love lavender fields! They're so...'

Ed jumped straight in to the space left by her hesitation. 'Provencal?'

She sighed, leaned towards him, and flopped a hand on his shoulder, wishing she hadn't quaffed quite so much of the carafe of wine when they'd stopped en route for dinner. 'Finishing my sentences for me now are we, Mitchum? Or should that be Mitch, given that it suits you so much better? Or maybe even Eddie?'

Not that she minded him finishing her sentences. Today there was something amusing about it, something playful, comfortable even.

'Call me anything you like, but definitely not Eddie.' He shot her an apologetic grimace, and screwed up his nose. 'The only person in the world who calls me Eddie is my mother. And I only do the sentence thing when you don't finish your own, Cinderella, which, by the way, suits you so much more than Millie when you insist on wearing dresses like this one.'

So he had noticed her dress. So far outside her budget, she really should have left it in the shop, but way too beautiful not to be bought. She tried not to think how this whole trip was whacking her finances to kingdom come.

In fact there was something so exceptionally alluring about the Provencal Ed (or should that be Mitch?) who'd met her at the airport, that she'd pretty much forgotten to find him annoying at all since she arrived, which was going to prove very useful, given what she had psyched herself up to be here for. Pulling a second foot up on the seat, she hugged both her knees tightly, trying to resist the dual shivers which that thought sent tingling down her spine.

Excitement and terror in equal measure, and all due to that bargain she'd made with herself when she'd been agonising about whether or not to come – that if she dared to get as far as boarding the plane, she was free of constraint for the weekend.

'Do you always put your feet on the car seats?'

She snorted as she picked up on his dirty look. Not a hundred percent un-annoying then, even in Provence.

And maybe she was showing an acre too much thigh here, regardless of her intended mission. Tugging hard at the shreds of skirt, she attempted to up the decency level, but one molten glare from Mitch told her she hadn't succeeded.

She shuffled, held her knees tighter, and gritted her teeth. 'It's comfy with my feet up, and it makes me feel secure, but if you object I'll put them down.' What had got into her? She'd have usually had a good go at Objectionable Ed for a comment like that, and here she was acquiescing. 'So long as you ask nicely that is.'

No need to abandon all principles, just because she'd decided to suspend her man-ban a teensy bit, as a celebration for being in Provence, for one weekend only.

Possibly.

And backing down already.

'Look, you'll see the Chateau coming into view as we skirt around the village, set slightly apart.'

She felt her mouth gape open as she took in the monumental stone walls, honeyed in the setting sun. 'Amazing!'

'There are huge walled gardens around the other side where we'll be, and the tent's already there.'

'One tent?' Her voice faltered, despite her reckless, albeit short-term, abandonment of her life-plan.

'It's large, you won't have any worries, you'll see.'

Typical. *As if he could second guess her worries.*

He shot her a grin. 'We're sneaking in the back entrance, by the way.'

Huge gateposts, that put her in mind of her Grandmother's place in the north, then a graveled track, winding between bougain-villeas and roses, and lawns neat and green, like the ones in the miniature garden set she'd loved as a child. Ed slung the car to a halt behind a low building, covered in climbing wisteria, and Millie's chest constricted in a series of jumps with each click of the handbrake ratchet.

Oh lordy!

'This is the pool house.' He was out of the car, already completely at home. Waving his arms, relaxed as his bare feet in his boat shoes, and horribly sexy in faded jeans that seemed low slung beyond the point of decency. 'There's a bathroom and a kitchen in there we can use.'

'Brill.' She replied, not taking her eyes off of him. Scarily sexy. But that's what she was here for.

'And here's the accommodation.' He led the way around the corner, grinning at her over his shoulder as a large, faded tent came into view. 'It's a vintage field tent that belongs to the Chateau, which the caretaker insisted we used, and it comes complete with vintage accessories.' He pulled back the flap, and dipped inside.

Millie tentatively followed him in. 'Oh my, it's like something from an interiors magazine! Someone thought of everything – rush matting on the floor, and even a tilting mirror! I never had a tent with one of those before.' She breathed in the smell of oiled canvas, and fingered one chunky hewn supporting pole, as she took in two beautiful caned lounging chairs. 'When you said camping, I never imagined anything like this.'

Running her eyes around, she caught a chest of drawers, with assorted bottles and glasses on top, next to a turned wooden clothes rail. Two camp beds, with crossed legs, one at each side of the tent, already made up, each with a filmy mosquito net suspended from the roof ridge. A neat pile of stripy quilts on a stool at the foot of each.

'It's a tent. Just not quite the pop-up variety.'

'It's amazing. So...' She swallowed back the word 'romantic', and this time he didn't jump in to finish her sentence. 'So evocative. It's lovely.'

'The beds are more comfortable than they look. They're high to combat the drafts, because vintage tents don't have a sewn-in ground sheet.' He kicked off his shoes, wriggled his feet into flip flops that were already sitting under one of the beds. 'I settled in earlier as you can see. Fancy a drink? I can recommend the rough red.'

Two camp beds? Rigorously single.

What the heck happened to the no-strings sex she'd come all this way for?

Her heart-rate slowed noticeably.

More to the point, what the hell had happened to Mr Sex-on-legs and his seduction techniques?

She swallowed an involuntary sigh. 'Yep, red would be great.'

So this was what he meant before when he said she wouldn't have any worries.

'All okay for you?' He scooped up glasses and a bottle, and headed for the flap.

'Everything perfect. Thanks. Couldn't be better.' She heard her own voice, a tiny bit flattened.

So that would be disappointment then.

***

Watching him light the lanterns around the terrace a few minutes later, she settled back against the cushions on her lounger, forced herself to sip her wine, and resisted the immediate urge to throw it back and score herself an instant courage boost.

'The light goes quickly here.' He sat down, stretched out his recliner, and languidly crossed one foot over the other. 'So here's to a weekend without rain.' He raised his glass and his eyebrows, sent her a lazy wink she didn't fully understand, and took a drink.

'The stars are already very bright.' Millie scanned the sky innocently, as slowly, and deliberately, she crossed her own legs. 'Like a Van Gough painting.' Trailed a lazy finger up an accidental-on-purpose patch of bare thigh.

Noted Ed's narrowed eyes glued to her finger.

Keep calm, and drink slowly.

Then nab your man.

No way was she going to let herself return home without jumping him.

There was a whole weekend ahead of her. She could afford to take her time.

She was a Burlesque teacher, seduction was her business, and if his gaze on her leg was anything to go by, he was there for the taking, whatever he was pretending. Ultimately, she had the power to make him do exactly what she wanted, when she wanted, and she'd do well to remember that, although when she stopped to analyse it, he'd given very little of himself away this far. Possibly because she hadn't taken the time to ask.

'So, tell me how you set up all these fireworks then?' She offered a softening smile. 'Do we need to save the empty wine bottle?'

Starting by getting him to talk. When his reply came it had just the amount of wounded indignation she'd anticipated.

'It's not just about propping rockets in bottles you know.'

She did know, very well, but she was happy for him to tell her anyway. Happy to sit and let his dark voice drift over her in the balmy night air, as he explained the intricacies of triple breaking shells, ignition procedures and software-aided choreography. Enjoying the way he took pains to describe it to her, made sure she understood, infecting her with his unbridled enthusiasm for all things explosive. Only an hour and a half later, as her prompts dwindled, and she stifled a yawn, did he show any sign of stopping.

'Time for bed?' He was smiling, looking her straight in the eye, and not a hint of flirtation or ambiguity, dammit. 'We've an early start in the morning. I'll let you use the bathroom first.'

Full steam ahead to single beds then?

Millie ground her teeth. She'd been lured here under false pretences. No way was she bringing out the full blown seduction yet, but she'd make darned sure this wasn't easy for him.

When Ed came back to the tent from the bathroom, Millie was sitting cross legged on her camp bed, in a vest and tiny shorts, brushing her hair. Knowing, simply from the way he sucked in a breath as he pushed through the entrance flap, that he was reacting. Not that she made a habit of hanging herself out there, but this guy deserved to be brought off the fence, big style.

She threw out a line. 'Any chance you could help me sort this mosquito net?'

Sensing his hesitation, she concentrated on the distant noise of cicadas outside, overlaid now with the deep thud of his heart, resonating across the space between them.

'Of course, no problem.' Grating as a gravel-pit, and, at a guess, he was lying. Hugely.

And totally underestimating how she'd react herself, how much she wanted him, now she was sitting here, barely dressed.

Dragging in one long ragged breath, she pushed herself to standing, trembling slightly. He raked his eyes over her, swallowed hard, still in his jeans, and the dark thrust of his erection giving him away like nothing else could.

'Get into bed.' His low rasp was determined. '*Then* I'll sort the mosquito net.'

Point taken. Off the fence, in anyone's book. And given her mission for tonight was done, she should be doing as he requested, except she wasn't. She couldn't walk away, not now, because her legs wouldn't work like that. Instead she found herself crossing the floor towards him, the rush matting smooth under her bare feet, the scent of clean man, warm skin, wrapping itself around her head as she drew closer. Reaching up to touch, she stretched out a hand, aching to feel the roughness of his jaw against her palm.

'Millie...' Chiding now, warning, he circled her wrist with strong, resistant fingers.

And just as she'd braced herself to be wrenched away from him he hesitated, turned to bury his face in her hand, ran his lips along her inner arm, all the way to the crook of her elbow, his stubble sending a scale of notes tumbling through the tender skin that left her legs quaking.

Then he grasped her hand again, spun her swiftly around, and led her firmly back towards her bed. 'Get in...'

'Why?' Feeling like a sulky child being ordered around, and no doubt she sounded like one.

'Get in, because I need to talk to you.'

'Why waste time talking?' Anger, and disappointment writhed in her chest. He'd pushed her away again, and suddenly she didn't care how belligerent she sounded. 'You're the one who suggested the no-strings sex. What the hell happened to majoring on pleasure? Not meaning to be rude, but there's firm evidence to suggest you're up for it, so why back off now?'

'I need to be sure you can handle it.' He pulled in a juddering breath. 'Maybe you're not as empowered as I thought. Sorry to sound boring, but I need to know it isn't going to hurt you a whole lot more than you're already hurt.'

How the hell did he know she was hurt? 'You don't have any idea what you're talking about.'

'Well that's fine. Let's leave it there then.'

She opened her mouth, thinking to explode, then closed it again. All the way to frigging Provence, and he says leave it there? How about no? If there'd been a proper ceiling she'd have been bouncing off it. From the closed down look on his face he was serious. Surely not?

'So you're saying no sex without a preliminary talk?'

Before she'd been wavering about whether to go through with

it, but his flat denial made her know she wanted it. Badly.

He nodded. 'That's about it. Your choice.'

She shifted on the camp bed, which creaked loudly, and gave an inward groan ten times louder than the complaining bed frame.

'Okay. So what do you want to know?' Keeping her cool here. *Straight forward seduction would be so much simpler.*

'You can start by me telling me about the guy.'

The guy? Her stomach crunched. 'Which guy?'

'Don't make this difficult. The one who hurt you.'

She clenched her teeth, beat her fists against her thighs in frustration. And then she gave in. Ever so slightly.

'He was called Josh.'

'And?' Ed caught hold of a quilt from the end of the bed. 'Here, you lie down, I'll sit on the floor. Jeans permitting.' He gave a momentary grimace. 'It'll be easier like that. At least for me.'

As she turned onto her side, put her head on the pillow, the light cover spilled over her, then he stooped to fold himself cross-legged on the floor. Flopped one arm casually across her hip, just like that. Easy and comfy. She could have stayed like that forever.

'Okay. So who the hell was Josh?'

She started, as he spat his question through gritted teeth.

'Sorry.' He corrected himself quickly, spoke more reasonably this time. 'Who was Josh?'

She raised her eyebrows, sucked in a sigh.

'Josh and I went out for a couple of years that was all.' Play it down. No need to say he was her first real boyfriend and that they'd gone out for four years.

'A couple of years?'

'Okay, three. Four maybe.'

'Your first proper relationship?'

She, nodded, then regretting it, turned on him. 'What is this – interrogation?'

He rolled his eyes. 'No, I simply want to understand why you're still in pieces, how many years down the line did you say it was?'

'I didn't.' She flipped him a dirty look, for pretending to know what she'd hadn't told him. 'It's two years since we broke up.'

He shifted, the pressure of his arm on her hip, shifting to her waist. She shifted in turn beneath it.

'So, tell me more about him.' Prompting, coaxing now. 'What was he like, what did he do?'

'We were both at uni, and on the face of it, he had it all. He was clever, good looking, had more money than he knew what to do with, and charm by the bucketful.'

Missing out the bits about the fast, rich, lifestyle, about being the golden couple everyone wanted to be like, meant to last forever.

Ed sniffed, flashed her a rueful grin. 'Getting the picture, and I already hate him.'

'That's why the stuff you do is such a blast. With Josh it was all about impressing people, all about how big, how much. All meaningless, all empty. It's been so cool to do real things, with a real, grounded, honest person, just for a short time. It kind of showed me what matters, what I should look out for, when I finally decide to settle down.'

Ed cleared his throat, appeared to be examining the floor at length.

There, she'd even embarrassed him by saying that, that was the kind of nice guy he was.

'Settling down being decades in the future. Obviously.' Adding that in, just so he was clear.

Eventually he looked up again. 'So why did you break up?'

'The first time I asked anything of him he ran out on me. I needed him to be there for me, and he melted away. Legged it. It was a horrible shock.' She expected her voice to crack, but was surprised to hear the words, flat and without emotion.

'I can imagine.'

Lucky he could, because no way would she share the awful details, not with anyone, ever.

She moved on swiftly. 'At the time I thought he loved me, but afterwards I realised he wasn't capable of loving anyone but himself. That he had nothing whatsoever to give to anyone else. It was my mistake, I chose the wrong guy.'

'And that's what stopped you trusting people?'

'Yep. Being let down, by someone you love is the worst feeling, and I'd rather not risk it again.' Strange to talk about it now, dismissing all that pain in a few simple sentences.

He studied her thoughtfully. 'And are you over him?'

'Over him personally, yes.' And somehow, as she spoke it out loud to Ed, she knew for certain for the first time, that she was over Josh, and the revelation sent a flutter through her stomach.

'Over the whole experience?'

She shrugged, turned her mouth down at the corners, knowing it was something she wouldn't ever get over. 'Ask me again in five years.'

'Not everyone is like him, Millie.' He shook his head, sadly she thought. 'And hopefully you've learnt from it.'

She let her face break into a rueful grin. 'I learned two good rules for life. One, I want to be self-reliant, and two, I'll never to go within ten miles of a rich guy.'

She heard him let out a hollow laugh, as he sprung to his feet. 'Make sure you stick to that then, but you'd better watch out – most men in Provence are loaded.'

One fleeting pat on her shoulder, and he'd backed away.

Two minutes later, he'd arranged her mosquito net, turned down the light, and she heard the creak of his own camp-bed as he got in.

And that was that.

CHAPTER SEVEN

BOWLING through the morning sun towards Avignon, in the under-powered hire car, and Ed had decided surviving the weekend was going to be a whole heap easier if he made sure there were obstructions between him and Millie.

Physical obstructions.

Like the table at breakfast, the gear stick now, the thirty glorious miles of no-man's-land he'd have put between them, when he'd dropped her in town, and he was back in the village sorting out the final preparations for tonight's display. Because without physical barriers, he was having one hell of a job keeping his hands off her.

And hands off was how it had to be.

One lucky break then, that he'd hit on the idea of talking. When they talked it kept her a. occupied, b. still, and, c. – this far at least – out of his danger zone.

'So what about your family?' He threw out an easy opener, designed to guarantee trouble-free conversation, so long as he didn't allow her to flip the subject onto him.

Jumping at his question, just a little, but she composed herself for a quick reply.

'We're pretty normal really. Mum, Dad, three girls. I guess the main thing that made us different was my sister being ill. I'm the middle child. Middle children are meant to go wild, as a way of grabbing some attention, and I didn't disappoint on that score.'

'And still rebelling now?' He was trying to avoid looking at her, but he broke convention to flash her a grin, then instantly regretted it when he was rewarded with her dazzler of a smile that turned his guts to butter.

'You noticed then.' She chortled. 'Old habits – can't give 'em up. But seriously, it was hard having a sister who was ill. We just got on with it, but looking back my parents were eaten up with the caring and the hospitals and the anxiety, and it was normal that any energy they had left went to my younger sister. She's always going to stay the baby, however old she gets. I was left to myself a lot. I spent hours on my own, making things, painting and drawing, but that's what I went on to do at uni, so it wasn't all bad.'

A very optimistic view, given how wobbly she'd been the other day about her family.

'And what about sibling rivalry. Did you fight?' Padding it out here, but hell, he needed to, given that Avignon was still miles away. He was also tentatively searching for common ground, because where sibling rivalry was concerned, he was an expert.

'You aren't supposed to fight with ill kids, and there's huge pressure to be nice to them, but I was insanely jealous of my older sister. Couldn't help it. The younger one was pretty much in the same boat as me.'

And good to meet a fellow sufferer.

'Do you see them much?'

'Now and again. My mother hates my tattoos.'

That would be a plural there, so he was right, it wasn't just the tendrils on her leg. He allowed himself a private smirk of congratulation, and a swift glimpse at her shin as she carried on.

'Let's say my parents are still coming to terms with who I've chosen to be, how I live my life. I'm sure we'll get there. Eventually.' Out of the corner of his eye he saw her shrug diffidently. 'So how about you. Tell me about your family?'

Damn. Too busy smirking to see that deflection coming. 'My family is large, complex, and better not talked about.' Just about covered the whole goddam nightmare of it. 'But I've been thinking about what we talked about last night.'

Avoidance tactics. Go on the offensive.

'And?'

'I wondered what made you decide to ditch your life-plan.'

He could see by the way she chomped on her lip, the question had stopped her in her tracks, then made her wind most of today's skirt around her fingers.

'Are you wearing shorts under there?' An emergency enquiry, best to check, before she induced a full-blown heart attack.

'Obviously.'

Except it wasn't obvious at all or he wouldn't have asked.

'Although technically these are knicker shorts. They're thinner for the heat, with a bit of lace, but they do the same job.' She looked puzzled. 'So what's that got to do with my life-plan?'

Ed concentrated hard to banish all thoughts of Millie's bits of lace, and failed miserably.

'Well, as I understood it, there was no space in your life for majoring on pleasure, or any man who might make that happen, and suddenly, last night, there you were, hell bent on talking your way into my bed. So what changed?' He allowed himself one glance her way, to max out the way those lovely, full lips parted in shock, then sat back to wait.

Not expecting a fast response, he had to swallow his own surprise when she came right back at him.

'I gave it a lot of thought, and decided to make an exception, for one time only. First, because you promised you'd be leaving, second, because for two years I've been trying to make myself emotionally self-reliant, and I thought sex with you would be a good test of how far I'd come.' Only the way she was chewing the life out of her thumb nail now gave any indication she wasn't supremely confident. 'You see, for me temporary is good. I wouldn't have considered it at all without that temporary guarantee, and somehow I knew you wouldn't mind being the guinea pig here. So what do you think?'

Not sure how to take the whole the guinea pig thing, but the rest was convincing him that she'd thought this one out, and might be strong enough to enjoy it after all. Just the once, on their very last date, which according to Cassie's rules was Date Ten, not forgetting he still had to meet both families. And as this weekend was clocking in as Date Seven, that was still a hell of a long way down the line, adding up to one hell of a lot of temptation to resist.

'I think you might have swung it.' Spinning her an encouraging beam, because it was way too early for the wicked grin he wanted to deal her. 'One last thing.' He was clutching frantically for delaying tactics here. 'Before we move on to major on pleasure, you need to dance for me first.'

Counting to five, bracing himself, time for her to take a breath and hit the stop button.

'No way!'

Fired like a bullet from a gun, and landing right on target.

He pursed his lips to contain his smirk of self-congratulation. 'Can I ask why not?'

'Dancing's private. It's a girl thing.'

That one made him splutter, loudly, even though he was ultimately in favour of her declining.

'Your Santa Baby client's going to show her dance to a man I presume. As his Christmas gift, and a very nice one too. I approve of gifts like that.'

The determined set of Millie's jaw was encouraging. 'One big difference, the Santa Baby guy isn't temporary.'

He heaved a mental sigh of relief, and thanked his lucky fire-works she liked arguing. She wasn't about to back down on this one any time soon.

'Well, this is Avignon coming up, so it looks as though we'll have to continue this discussion later.'

'This isn't up for discussion Ed, this one's non negotiable.' Belted straight back at him, with a force that took even an explosives expert by surprise.

Better and better.

He wasn't entirely sure how many dates he could spin this one out for. Millie was gritting her teeth now, and she had an un-nerving habit of caving when he least expected, but anything was a bonus, and if he played this right, the hands-off scenario would be a given for this whole weekend. Biting his lip now, to keep his face from splitting into a grin the width of the horizon, whooping silently, and doing a mental high-five. He had scored himself a safe pass. The pressure was off.

Except then she bent down to pull her handbag off the car floor, sending a whole wave of woman scent powering into his face, and he knew by the way his stomach hit the deck that as far as she was concerned, for him the pressure would never be off.

Because simply being near Millie Brown sent his libido quietly and inexorably crazy.

***

Early evening, and the whole village was heaving as Ed wound his way through the narrow streets, dodging the moneyed, sun-varnished visitors who had flocked to be seen against the backdrop of the picturesque evening market, milling in readiness for the fireworks later. Picking up Millie from Avignon had gone better than expected. As anticipated, the volume of her shopping bags was a serious challenge for the rental car – a truck would have been a better option. But the good news was she'd barely paused for breath as she animatedly filled him in on the day's exploits and purchases, and they'd grabbed something quick to eat at a roadside cafe – *thank you Cassie*. Then he'd dropped her at the tent, mumbled something about showers, and fled.

Sorting out a firework display had to be a good enough excuse for anyone.

Except he knew the guys could handle things perfectly without him hanging around, like they always did when he was off on bigger, more exciting projects, and he didn't want to tread on their toes now. Sentimental he was not, but he'd been coming to his parents' chateau here longer than he could remember. The Mitchum family had been making an annual donation to the village to cover the costs of the summer fireworks for years before he got into the firework business, and although he'd always secured the contract on his own merits, it was a matter of honor to put on a stunning show every year. Somewhere down the line the summer festival fireworks in the village were as much of a calendar-marker for him as Christmas, and taking responsibility for the design of this show by turning up to work alongside the guys was something he'd always held on to, regardless of his growing work commitments elsewhere.

But right now the guys didn't need him. And he knew he was stalling. Staying as far away from Millie as he could, because the idea of shepherding her through the crowds, being forced to rub against the whole delicious smell of her, to press against the enticing heat of her, tied his gut into knots. He was one strong guy, but something told him that might tip him over the edge, and although he was cringing with guilt at running out on her like this, right now the few hundred yards between them just didn't seem like enough.

***

When Millie came out of the pool house after her shower later that evening, the long evening shadows on the garden were already smudging towards dusk. Ed had rushed off, no doubt to make last minute adjustments to his shell firing and ignition systems – oh yes, she had been listening last night – so she'd had no reason to hurry. She'd had a quick shuffle through her pile of shopping bags, knowing the real thrill would come when she opened them up again back home next week. She limited herself to extracting one star item from the bags to try on later, a gorgeous black vintage jacket, bought from a second-hand clothes stall, whose cut hugged her so close it had seemed like fate to find it waiting for her.

Shivering slightly despite the warm evening air, she ran her fingers through her hair as she scanned the distant smokey hills, thankful that she'd found a hair dryer in the shower room. She doubted she would ever earn enough to treat herself to a cut at the top London salon she used to go to so regularly when she'd accepted the allowance from her parents. How she'd taken that for granted. What she used to spend on haircuts alone would keep her going for months in the country up north. Picking up that mountain of shopping today in town had re-awakened an unsettling hunger for the urban buzz she craved. She ignored the niggle deep inside, spurring her on to get back to the city she loved. As much as she missed it she was certain she'd only go back on her own terms, as an independent woman, who supported herself.

One grimace allowed, but only if she buried those pangs. She looked at her bags. Mountain of shopping? Mountain range more like. Triple *Merci beaucoup*. One for cash machines and credit cards, two, for the pool house to store it in, and three, for Ed's offer to transport it all home in the company van. At least her visit hadn't been wasted, not that a visit to Provence was ever a waste, but her original premise for getting on the plane had gone right out of the window, when Ed had turned cooler than a polar bear's toe-nails.

One red hot guy who couldn't make up his mind, ready enough to talk about sex, dangle it tantalisingly in front of her, then whipping the offer away, and driving her wild into the bargain. Maybe it had only been her own wishful thinking to imagine it was ever on the cards.

And now, even keeping her at arm's length didn't seem enough. Today she'd noticed he'd been resorting to obstacles to keep her at bay. At the cafe he'd pretty much dived for the shelter of the table, and it had been the same at breakfast. In the tent he'd deftly circled behind the cane loungers. So much for majoring on pleasure. When a guy was hiding behind furniture to make sure you didn't jump him, maybe it was time to let go.

Except he had to be the best kisser in the world.

And although both were kisses which he'd broken, almost before they'd begun, she couldn't help imagine how the next bit would have been. She'd been doing it since the first day she woke up snogging him. It hadn't exactly become an obsession, but it did fill a large proportion of her waking hours and stopped her getting to sleep at night, especially when the man in question was in a creaking camp-bed, a scant two yards away from her.

Hitching up her towel, she headed towards the tent, vintage jacket in hand. Ed would be gone until after midnight, and that was hours away. She would wander into the village later, to watch the fireworks. They would surely be the only action she saw from Ed any time soon.

Back in the gloom of the tent, she lit the oil lamp, rifled through the camp chest of drawers for underwear, then slipped on the jacket. Tailored short, black, with a deliciously nipped in waist, she twisted in front of the mirror to admire it.

89

'Wow!' That forties cut worked wonders for a girl's rear view, but definitely called for heels. She grabbed the pair of precipitous courts she'd brought, which had seemed a regrettable waste of case-space when she'd seen the cobbled village streets, and twirled again, smoothing the silk over the curves of her hips. 'Oh, yes! Perfect.'

Had to be worth every Euro of debt.

'And I'll second that...'

One hoarse growl, that jolted her six inches into the air, and made her heart lodge somewhere in her throat. She'd have cried out, but her breath had whooshed away.

Her legs weakened as she caught Ed's shadowy reflection in the mirror.

'What..?' She let out one strangled squeak

'Sorry.' His broad shouldered sincerity spilled across the tent like melted chocolate, infusing her with warmth. 'I didn't mean to scare you.'

Hard to resist, but seeing how he'd practically given her a heart attack, he needed telling all the same. 'You shouldn't...'

She turned towards him, and the molten lust in his eyes clamped the words in her throat.

'What – creep up on people?' His low laugh resonated, as he came towards her. 'Pleased I did. I'd have hated to miss out on these lacy shorts! Cinderella, this time without a dress! Just what the doctor ordered!'

This was not how she'd meant to be seen.

Her stomach disintegrated beneath his gaze, which rolled up her now, smoldering over her acres of exposed leg, making every nerve in her body jangle.

'I'll grab a skirt.' She ran her fingers through her hair distract-edly. So necessary, but a bit of a bluff, given that her feet were rooted to the spot.

'No, don't.' He hesitated, his drawl hoarse, as his lips twitching into the slightest of smiles. 'Stay as you are. I like you like that.'

Her breaths juddered, as she took in the determined set of his jaw, her eyes fluttering down to the jeans stretched tight over his hips, and the aching bulge of his not so low-slung arousal.

'I was trying on the jacket I bought.' She tried to hide behind a light, every-day tone.

'Lucky I came by when I did then.' He tilted his head, observing her through narrowed, amused eyes. 'And here's me thinking you were getting ready to give me the dance you promised.'

Indignation at the cheek of him rushed through her, whooshing away her shakes. 'Excuse me! I didn't promise you anything! And you know it!'

Another of his low laughs, and a pulse of shivers radiated through her. He took one more pace towards her, and the same distinctive scent that had been haunting her dreams engulfed her, delectable yet indefinable, vaporised by the hottest male skin.

She jumped again, as his touch landed light on the side of her leg. Barely there, tracing. Sending inexplicable spasms of desire spiraling through her.

'Do you never stop arguing?' Laughing again, he stretched to push her hair back from her face, and rubbed one broad thumb over her cheek, dissolving her bones instantaneously. 'I'm teasing Millie, I'm the one who made the promises, if I remember rightly.'

If he was talking about the majoring-on-pleasure promise, she was happy to let him off.

One thumb, rubbed across her face, and already in pieces.

What the hell happened to Millie – I'm-here-to-jump-Ed-Mitchum – Brown?

If her legs hadn't turned to jelly, this was the point when she'd have run. Except now, she couldn't move at all, unless, perhaps if she collapsed completely.

She heard herself gulp, as he put one finger under her chin, and tilted it upwards.

Then his tanned, beautiful face was heading towards her. One blurry moment later his hot sensuous mouth was over hers, and as her heart exploded she remembered exactly why she was here.

CHAPTER EIGHT

MILLIE parted her lips and gave herself up to drink in the whole glorious familiar taste she'd craved so badly. As the waves of pleasure flooded over her, she knew this was achingly familiar, yet scarily different. When she finally broke away, it was only to steady herself, to drag in some oxygen, because when he was this close, the air she breathed didn't seem to work any more. With both the other kisses she'd been the initiator. But this time he was in control. It was his choice, his roaring libido that was driving him if the fearsome plunder of her mouth was anything to go by. Like everything she'd been dreaming, only so much better, so much stronger, so much more compulsive.

She staggered as her fingers clenched the soft fabric of his t-shirt, snagging it away from the powerhouse of his neck, exposing a collarbone that flipped her stomach with its vulnerability. Kneading the flexing muscles of his shoulders, she looked up into his face. The simple tautening of the hollows beneath his cheekbones sent electric spasms through her and made her knees sag further. She leaned in, finding support against the hard planes of his chest, heard his feral groan as she accidentally forged her hip against the ridge of his erection

'Are you still breathing?' His concern resonated in her ear, as he grazed his teeth lightly along her neck, sending a seismic wave of desire shuddering through her.

'I'm breathing, just.' Reading the depth of his need from the fogging of his eyes.

'Good.' One slick movement, he'd undone the buttons of her jacket. Then his hand slid up her rib-cage, to cup her breast. 'Oh yes...'

Taking from his groan of appreciation, he liked what he'd found.

Her vision slid into soft-focus as he flipped down her bra cup, rubbed her nipple teasingly, but tortuously to attention, releasing a whole ocean of molten desire to pool between her legs. 'Oh yes.' Her own guttural response, echoed, as if from a distance.

'Oh yes.' Again. Driving her wild as he set to work on the other nipple, capturing the first with his mouth, grazing, sucking, biting, his dark hair tousled below her chin. All she could do was to stand, eyelids faltering as she teetered on her heels, cross-eyed with the doubling of the pleasure tracks, legs parted as she arched instinctively, winding herself towards the nerve centre of his erection, willing him to satisfy some aching, building, burning chasm of need that was building within her. After everything in the past she'd worried it might be difficult, but it wasn't difficult at all, it was staggeringly, awesomely easy.

Now he trailed a finger from her knee to her thigh, hooked the elastic of the leg of her shorts, turned her inside out as he plunged deep into her slippery wetness, exploring the depths of her as she angled herself to make the most of his delectably probing fingers. Only the burn of stubble on her breast pulled her momentarily back to reality, to the stuttering flicker of the oil lamp, the tumbling cascade of her clothes spilling out of the open drawers. And the fleeting worry, that he might notice when she didn't come. The big elusive O was something she rarely reached. No big deal. Coming just wasn't her thing.

Losing it again, as his fingers sucked from her depths, and

emerged, found the nub of her sex, and turned the near distance to a blur of white noise with one flick.

'You know I'm going to have to take your shorts off soon.' Ed's low laugh, vibrated hot against her ear, as he buried his face in her neck.

'Yeah, but don't stop doing...' Her own moan, desperate. Knowing she needed him right where he was, doing exactly what he was doing. Nothing more, nothing less. Thrusting herself against him now, and the pleasure and the pressure inside her building like a mountain. A totally unfamiliar place she didn't recognise, but knowing she had to go there anyway. And suddenly he was pushing her over some invisible edge, and she was falling. Falling. Falling, like falling off a wall, and there was nothing she could do about it. Then an exploding cascade of heat and colour shot through her body, carrying her with it, in wave after glorious wave, thrilling her and choking her at the same time. And from very far away she heard her own agonised moans, like a distant out-of-body experience. It was a long time later, when she finally came to rest at the bottom of the mountain again.

Pushing damp hair off her forehead, clinging to his shoulders, shuddering with aftershocks, dragging desperate gulps of air.

'Hey. You okay?' In his gravelly voice, she heard one tenth concern, nine tenths satisfaction.

Okay? How about a million times better than okay.

'Oh lo-o-rd' Even her voice was staggering.

So that was what all the fuss was about. And if that was a proper big O, the minor, faltering O's she'd struggled to grasp before weren't even worthy of the name.

'Thanks.' She shot a broad grin in his direction, knowing however wide, it couldn't begin to cover her gratitude. 'That was amazing.'

'As promised. We aim to please.' He let out another low laugh.

'All that heat, and more! Who'd have thought it? So, where to next?'

'Sorry? How do you mean?'

His low growl grazed her ear. 'Shall we go inside or out? To finish.'

Knowing she was opening and closing her mouth, totally incapable of decisions at this point.

'Moving this along,' he cut in, swiftly, 'outside's as private as in. You can look up at the stars.'

'What?' Mega orgasms or not, she wasn't letting him get away with that one. 'So you just assumed you're going on top?'

'Okay, *we* can look up at the stars. Come on Cinderella.' He grasped her hand, grabbed some quilts from the pile by the bed, and a moment later they were on the terrace.

The night air brought her to her senses, stopping her dead. 'Do you have protection?'

She had the pregnancy thing covered, but seeing how he liked to max out with no-strings...

'Damn. You've caught me out there – one scout in a tent, who's not prepared!' He flicked her an embarrassed grimace. 'Mine are buried in the pool house somewhere.'

So maybe this wasn't exactly what he'd planned.

'No worries, I'll sort it.' One dash, as fast as her heels would allow, to the supply in her bag, bought in a bullish moment at the airport, never truly believing she'd get to use them.

And here she was now. Running. Crazy for the next part.

By the time she returned, he'd lit a lantern or two, spread the quilts on the ground, and stripped off his shirt, to reveal a heart-stoppingly toned six-pack, that sent a flurry of nervous shivers beating through her stomach, then crazy, powering lust took over and stamped them into submission. Something about the way he was already sitting, long legs crossed casually in front of him sent a rocket of anticipation bursting through her.

'Come here, you.' He leaned backwards, propped himself on one elbow, and inclined his head, darkly. 'If you're sure you don't want a view of these wonderful Provencal stars, you'd better lose your shoes, and take a seat.'

***

As he stretched out his hand to meet hers, the scent of her on his fingers from before drifting on the night air, cranked his already bursting erection up, yet another notch. As if that was possible. He was fully aware that doing this right now could surely wreck his game plan, but completely unable to stop himself. As soon as he'd stumbled into the tent and found her, all legs and heels and achingly sexy shorts, he'd known he was a goner.

'Condoms.' She leaned, slipped two packs into his pocket, and as he caught a front-of-house view of those full, luscious breasts, he kicked himself for ever being hooked on svelte partners.

Some things amped a man too much to resist, and Millie in underwear, tight jacket splaying over her breasts and hips sent him to the stratosphere, and the way she'd fallen into that orgasm before, was something else. He was heading for a mega-shell explosion here, and if it wrecked his challenge, well, hell, that was just too bad. Some things were worth the sacrifice, and this had to be one of them.

'Come here you...' He eased her down to sit astride his stomach. He winced as she landed too far back, giving his erection a forceful nudge. Excruciating. Much more of that and it would be over before it began.

Easing back to lying now, loving the way her pouting lips parted and her smokey eyes widened as she settled onto him, drinking in the sticky scent of her arousal. Wishing he was more in control, because Mr Cool was in danger of losing it here.

Her jacket parting, as he cupped those breasts through her bra, each a heavy over spilling handful, whipping down the bra cups to unleash them, toying with the pouting nipples until she moaned, and thrashed. One woman, with animal responses like he'd never seen, and turning him on like nothing else, ever.

He slipped his hand inside her pants, sensing her disintegrate as he slicked his fingers. 'Time to lose the shorts?'

Wordlessly, she stood, peeled them off, then crouching beside him, and began to ease down his zip.

'No wait.' The zap from one pull from her on his zipper, almost sending him over the edge. He was going to have to unzip himself here. 'Still sure you want me to look at the sky?'

Watching her nod, silently, as he peeled his jeans off, rolled his protection on. Whatever the lady wanted... Noting the wild flaring of her eyes as she saw exactly what he had to offer, which felt like its usual extra large, plus a whole, whole lot more, every expanded inch of it down to her.

'Well, me in the star-gazer position, means you're going to have to serve yourself here...'

Telling it like it is. Just not expecting her take on that one, and jumping, violently, as she ran one tracing finger tip along his length, again, as she gripped his shaft.

'No.' Firmly taking her hand away. 'I need you to sit on me, Millie.' His most persuasive, urgent smile, lost somewhere between the dark and the unbearable ache of his arousal. 'Like now, would be good...'

With a hand on each thigh, he urged her hips towards his face. Tilted her backwards, buried his mouth, and tasted the whole salty creaminess of her, as his tongue found her nub. So darned easy to arouse, already forging into him. He'd promised her a pleasure max and that was what he'd give her. Hearing her kitten-soft moans grow urgent as he licked, and tangled, sucking until she rolled and roared. Had to be the sexiest thighs he'd had clamped around his head, ever. Her movements as she fell into a climax, turning him on like he couldn't imagine. And him, busting and throbbing, holding it together, just.

'She shook her head dazedly, drew stuttering gasps. 'That was crazy.'

'Crazy good?' Not looking for compliments, just checking.

'You bet.'

Sliding her backwards as he waited for her to breathe again, then he slicked a thumb across his mouth, and pulled her into one kiss, deep as a river. Guiding her hips backwards, nudging her towards him, and edging her onto his own straining erection, which felt huge enough to be grazing the sky. Watching her eyelids faltering as she pulled her mouth away, hearing her one sharp cry as he entered her. Easing her downwards, trying to resist the incredible pleasure of it, and trying to slow the bang of his heart.

Up to the hilt now.

'This is going to be fast.' Grating out his excuses, as he spurred her into a rhythm, forged into her incredible tightness. Finding her nipples, grazing them as she writhed, then, as she folded above him, and when he knew he couldn't hold much longer, a final flick of her clitoris, sent her convulsing around him. Only then did he allow himself to let go. One ecstatic thrust, all it took, to propel him into the most body-shattering orgasmic bang of his life.

***

'So, I'm guessing the no-strings thing lets you to put your arm around me then?'

Ed, relaxing, naked on the quilt, pushed himself up on an

elbow, took in his offending arm, strewn lazily across the curve of Millie's waist, and rolled his eyes to the star-spattered sky above.

The fact she had suspended her questioning long enough for sex to take place at all, was starting to seem like a minor miracle. Whilst he was happy to drift into an easy post-coital slumber, only spoiled by the grumbles of thunder rolling around the distant hills, which he was determinedly ignoring, Millie had snapped into a post-coital frenzy.

'It's fine for me to put my arm around you.' He sighed, dug deep for patience. Only Millie could make something as straight-forward as no-strings *this* complicated. 'The way it works, I'm all yours for the weekend. Just not for forever.'

She rolled out from under his arm, and spun him an unapologetic smile as she twisted to sit. 'I like to get these things straight, that's all.'

Not yet back in her shorts, and delightfully, not giving a damn. Jacket still open. And not her fault her pout was irresistible.

His plans in tatters, and given the fire he'd just lived through, he wouldn't have had it any other way.

No regrets.

Nor was it her fault, the way her thighs were lush, and splashed with moonlight. Already turning him hard again. Maybe the best way to calm them both down was to take her once more time.

'Getting things straight is good.' He shot her a grin as wicked as he felt. 'So, if we're sorting stuff out here, next time, will you get to look at the stars?'

'There's going to be a next time?'

Reaching out, starting at her ankle bone, he absently traced a finger up the wandering tendrils of her tattoo. 'I should say. Wouldn't you?'

'I guess.' She chewed her thumbnail pensively, and narrowed her eyes. 'As for who goes on top, maybe I'll fight you for it.'

'And maybe you won't.' Pulling himself up to sitting now, tugging her to sit astride him, grunting gently as a load of warm woman landed right on target, shuffled herself onto the hub of his erection. 'This way we both get the same view of the sky.'

And she wasn't fighting now.

Two seconds, and he'd pushed back her jacket, pulled down her bra cups, and she'd entwined her arms around his neck and yanked her full breasts tight against his chest.

Warm? Hot, more like.

Legs locked around his back, her mouth burying into his with all the finesse of a heat seeking missile.

'Condom...' One last lucid thought, as he fumbled to find the pocket of his discarded jeans. 'Sorted.'

Then the lust-haze took over. One tilt of her pelvis and he'd powered deep inside her. Then she was riding, sliding him, grinding him, devouring him, thrashing him, and he was driving, pushing, thrusting relentlessly against her sweat slicked skin. One soft moan in her throat, which built to an animal cry, and she was rigid in his arms, then all hell broke loose, as she contracted onto him in wave after wave of electrifying spasms, and as his blood roared through his ears, he surged into one, explosive release.

***

Much later, he woke to find her, damp and hot, crushed against his chest, on the quilt where they had fallen. Burying his face in the nest of her hair, breathing in the scent of her scalp, he was enveloped by a sudden crazy need to keep her close. Soft, silent, almost indiscernible, like the night breeze in the bougainvilleas, something making him want to reach out, hang onto the sky, and stop the world from turning.

Just for tonight.

Then one crashing boom burst through his head, and echoed across the horizon.

Mille jolted to life in his arms.

Then another crash, followed by a relentless volley of crackling shots.

'Fireworks!' He opened his eyes, scanned the dishes of cascading sparks radiating across the sky. 'Cripes!'

No idea where the last two hours went.

'Shouldn't you be...' She mumbled into his chest, pushing to free herself. 'Be somewhere else? With your box of matches?'

Good point, well made.

'No, it's fine. The team's got it sorted. ' He pushed himself up to sitting, he drew her to sit between his thighs. Speaking into her ear, to be heard over the explosions, suddenly secure with how she nestled into his chest, setting his heart speeding every time her back jarred against him with each extra-loud bang. As if the rise and fall of her breasts, heavy on his wrists, wasn't distracting enough. 'We're trying some new sequences tonight, so it'll all be filmed. My job is to watch.'

'From here?' Another explosion of colour across the heavens, another jump.

'Here will do.' Made him lock his arms tighter around her ribs, search out her hand. 'We don't get the backdrop of the Chateau, but the fireworks are the same.' He felt a shiver wobble through her.

'Cold?' He reached for a blanket, draped it over her legs.

'No.' She turned her face towards him in the dark, crushed her lips across his cheek, as she searched to find his ear to shout in. 'I think it's just the bangs.'

Making him smile. Making him want to dive into her mouth all over again. But he made himself resist, knowing he owed it to the guys to watch the show.

'What's this? A girl who doesn't like bangs?'

'No, it's loud but it's amazing! I love it!'

That response made his chest implode.

The bangs. Loud, resplendent, adrenalin-firing. But, for the first time in his life, he was finding them weirdly anticlimactic, given what had gone before. As they watched the mounting crescendo of glittering chaos above, Ed's gut flexed, not with each new flurry of light and explosion, but with each of Millie's enthralled cries. And right now he was counting his way through the sequences he'd designed, willing them to be over, so he could get back to those other mind-blowing bangs. Who would have thought haystack Millie would push him over the edge, robbing him of every last ounce of self control he had. He may have been resisting before, but he was thriving on the inferno now.

And what an inferno! Fierce and short-lived, exactly how he liked it, and he was confident this fire would be all burned by the end of the weekend.

The display had reached the quiet section before the final storm, and over the smaller fireworks, he could hear the murmurs of the distant crowd, echoes of the band. And then, clapping through the gloom, an almighty, un-scheduled clatter of thunder, had Millie leaping from the ground.

She held out her hand. 'It's raining.'

Rain was the last thing he needed. Maybe it would come to nothing.

Above them a waterfall of fireworks was cascading down the clouds now, as the Grand Finale built towards its war zone conclusion, but as the rain fell harder, they scrambled to their feet.

'Run for it!' Ed's voice rang out over the noise of the thunderclaps and explosions, as they grabbed the quilts and clothes, and hurled themselves for shelter of the tent.

Inside, despite the thudding rain, Millie's shiver was low enough for him to register as she dragged on a t-shirt in the shadows.

Damn. Double Damn. He grimaced as a large drip bounced off his forehead. There was no way they could stay here.

Damn Cassie too, and the way she always managed to be right.

'Not sure this old canvas is up to a full blown Provencal storm.' He braced himself for the next bit. 'The Chateau owners gave strict instructions to move into the Gardener's Cottage if there was any rain.' He banished the image of Cassie and her gloating smile from his head, as he took in the water already squelching up through the rush matting, and brushed another smattering splash off his arm. Jeez. 'Come on, grab your stuff and we'll go.'

About to play with fire of a different kind here, and here's to hoping he could pull this one off.

CHAPTER NINE

MILLIE woke, arms caught in a tangle of sheets, face jammed into a dreamy-soft pillow.

Where the heck..? She opened her eyes a crack, and grimaced, as the morning light filtering through partly opened shutters bounced up off the pale limestone floor and zapped her headache up a notch.

Of course! The cottage, the Chateau, the rain, all came flooding back.

What *had* she done last night? Maxing the pleasure? Total debauchery more like. *And totally amazing.* She closed her eyes tight, as if that was going to stop the X-rated pictures flashing through her brain. And the O's, which had always eluded her – last night there'd been so many she'd lost count! Gingerly she extended a tentative leg across the bed. Phew! A space. At least she didn't have to face him, straight away. But he could come back any time, so she needed to move fast. Dragging the sheet around her, ignoring the wobbles in her legs, she made a dive for the en-suite, and buried herself in the drench of the shower.

***

'Orange juice!'

Millie emerged from the bedroom, swathed in a bath-sheet, heading across the airy, luxurious living area, to what she hoped was the kitchen. After all, when they'd arrived last night Ed had said to help herself to anything here. Given that fifteen minutes of water hammering on her head had done very little to sort her floppy knees and fluttering pulse, not to mention her doubts, she was hanging all her hopes on an instant injection of vitamin C, and a sugar boost. Juice was what she needed, and fast! She'd just honed in on a humming fridge the size of New York, when she heard the click of a door out in the hall.

'Hellooooo...'

A woman's voice. Millie froze, hand in mid-air, as the voice spiraled down the hall. O lordy! Not Ed then, though she had an idea her heart would be clattering even more if it had been.

'Hello – Eddie – are you there?' The voice grew more persistent, as the footfalls on the stone floor drew closer.

Eeeeeek!

Millie drew the bath towel up under her chin, pushed a strand of damp hair off her forehead, and sucked in a huge breath. Too late now to kick herself for not dressing.

'Oh, my dear, I'm so sorry!' A sandy haired woman, with a gently speckled tan arrived in the doorway, her designer loafers saying as much as her accent, which reminded Millie of her mother's. From the way the woman's hands flew to clutch at the cluster of beads at her throat, Millie guessed that in shock terms they were on an equal footing.

'I had no idea. Do forgive me, I've just flown in from Antigua.' The woman ran her palms over taupe linen trousers, flashed Millie a warm but apologetic smile, and leaned towards her with a rueful shrug, lowering her voice. 'I've a feeling I'm not meant to be here!'

Millie suspected that this woman was rarely in the wrong, but something about the frankness of her confession put Millie at ease. She wrinkled her nose into a grin, and gave a guilty shrug. 'That makes two of us then.'

'Sorry?' The woman inclined her head to Millie in query.

'I'm not meant to be here either. I'm a kind of stow-away.' Easy, when shared with a fellow conspirator.

'Oh, I see.' The woman hesitated. Raised her eyebrows in a way that looked uncannily familiar to Millie. 'Are you with Eddie – I mean Ed?'

'Yes.' Millie nodded slowly, and watched a delighted beam spread across the other woman's face. 'Except I'm not officially on the fireworks team – he whisked me in under the radar! We were staying in a tent before the rain.'

'Better and better!' The woman clapped her hands. 'Sounds perfect! You have no idea how pleased I am to see you, or how long I've waited for this to happen.' In two swift strides the woman had crossed the kitchen to rest a light hand on Millie's arm. 'Make sure you enjoy your stay dear.'

Millie, confused, replied to the only part of the conversation she understood. 'Thank you. I will.'

The woman was backing across the kitchen now, only hesitating as she reached the door. 'Oh, and it's probably best not to mention I was here...' A shadow of anxiety dulled her radiance, but only momentarily. '...if that's okay with you?'

And obviously not expecting an answer to her question, because she was gone before Millie had time to reply.

***

Millie had pulled on some shorts and was heading towards the fridge when the click of the front door stopped her in her tracks again. 'Okay, only me! I've been to the bakery.' Ed's voice resonated down the hall.

No time for her heart to bang as he burst in, tossed a bulging bag of croissants down on the table, dropped a kiss on top of her head, and grabbed a cafetiere from the side.

'I thought you'd be in need of breakfast.' He torched her with a wide grin. 'Coffee?'

Nice subtle reference to last night there.

'Please.' She reached for the juice as a stop-gap.

And just the right amount of contact. Enough to acknowledge her, but not enough to knock her helpless into next week, although the sight of him skidding around the kitchen was doing that anyway. Mega-sexy. Already showered. Totally unfair he could look that good after so much sex and so little sleep, when she was wrecked. Re-aligning her thoughts to glasses, she opened a cupboard hopefully, but he was way ahead, deftly dropping two on the work surface in front of her.

'Mmmmm, mango and passion fruit. Nice!' She splashed out the juice, pushed his towards him, and took a slug herself, eyeing him over her glass as he piled the breakfast items onto a tray. 'Here's hoping it has huge powers of resuscitation!'

'If you need resuscitating, you only have to ask...' He shot her a lazy wink, with more than a hint of smolder, as he picked up the tray, kicked his way through the open garden door, and sauntered out onto the terrace.

Millie followed, blinking as she emerged into the sunshine, and flopped down at the table, in the dappled shade of the vine pergola.

'Help yourself to croissants, we can get something more substantial in later...' He broke off at the sound of scrunching on the gravel path, jumping up as a white-haired man appeared beyond the bougainvillea bushes. 'Damn, it's the Mayor, probably come to say thanks for the display. You carry on, I'll be back in a minute!' He handed her a coffee, then hurried off towards the visitor.

Millie bit into her croissant and watched. Judging by his exuberant gesticulations, the Mayor was pleased with Ed's fireworks. His booming compliments echoed around the garden.

'*Incroyable!*' She couldn't avoid hearing. '*Formidable!*' And she couldn't help understanding. 'Incredible! Amazing! Your parents should be very proud, as usual!'

Funny how easily she could still pick up the French her Grandmother had taught her. Her jaw stopped in mid chew. Parents?

The mayor was slapping Ed on the back enthusiastically.

So which parents would they be exactly?

The Mayor had Ed in a full-blown head lock now, as he rattled on, and her brain automatically translated. 'You may be a firework master, but to me you will always be the small boy from the Chateau.'

The small boy from the Chateau?

What! Millie's jaw and her croissant dropped simultaneously.

Surely she'd heard wrongly, misread the Technicolor scene playing out in front of her. Too much sun, too little sleep.

The Mayor, obviously about to leave, was sending her an acknowledging salute, a parting shout. 'He's turned out well, eh the smallest Marshall boy?'

So she wasn't mistaken.

The woman in the kitchen earlier? Looking for Eddie?

Only my mother calls me Eddie. That's what he'd said, yesterday, in the car.

Millie tried to swallow, but all her saliva had gone. How could she have been such an idiot...

The Mayor was sweeping off behind the bay bushes now and, Ed was wandering back. 'Glad he liked it, but he's a bit full-on for breakfast time!'

By the time he reached his chair Millie, teeth gritted, was ready for him. 'What the hell is going on here?'

He blinked, apparently in genuine confusion. 'Sorry?'

She wasn't buying that.

'When exactly did dusty Ed from the quarry, morph into Ed from the Chateau?' She speared him with her stare, added a glacial afterthought. 'Or would that be Eddie?'

He inclined his head, his eyes darkening as they narrowed in query. 'You understood what he said?' His tone was incredulous. 'But he was rattling on like the clappers.'

'You aren't the only French speaker in the world Ed. My Grandmother's French, remember?'

Ed hammered his fist onto his forehead, slowly, three times, as if collecting himself.

She fixed her eyes on the column of his neck, the rise and fall of his Adam's apple, definitely not thinking about its salty taste, of snagging that skin between her teeth last night.

Finally he gave a nonchalant shrug that made her bile boil, and looked her square in the eye. 'Okay, you've got me there, I'm from the Chateau! But it's no big deal.'

Another rich guy, smoothing over trouble. How was that familiar?

The lurch in her stomach that eye-lock caused wasn't going to stop her. 'I suppose the darned quarry's yours then too is it?'

His face twisted, and he hesitated, dragged in another deep breath. 'As it happens, yes. But there's no need to over-react'

One dismissal that set the fire in her guts ablaze.

'Nice work! Make this about me over-reacting! I wouldn't have even spoken to you if I'd known you were loaded, let alone come to Provence for the frigging weekend. And your stack of lies just proves your pedigree as one more rich waste-of-space!'

Lashing out, kicking herself for landing here at all. Crashing to her feet now, desperate to go, anywhere, away from him.

'Before you leave...'

The nerve of the man! She yanked to a halt by the kitchen door. 'What?'

'About your boxes...'

'And?' What the hell did her boxes have to do with anything?

'If we're talking home truths, I've remembered where I've seen one before. It's in my mother's study, made by an artist from London apparently.' He paused, apparently to polish his supercilious sneer to the max.

Millie's overworked jaw sagged for the umpteenth time that morning. 'What are you talking about?'

He rocked on his heels, broad shoulders back, thumbs hooked through his belt loops. Glowering big time.

'It isn't clever to rip off other people's work, Millie.'

***

Ed forced himself to down his coffee, then a second cup, even though he hadn't tasted either, and only then did he allow himself to saunter into the house. Not that he was looking for Millie, because he wasn't, but given that the kitchen and the living room were empty, he wandered towards the bedroom, and poked his head around the door. One room-wide clothes explosion.

How could one woman with one tiny piece of hand luggage create this mayhem? The invisible tourniquet that had clamped itself around his chest slackened a notch. At least now he knew she hadn't run out on him completely. *Yet.* Looked like she hadn't even taken her handbag. He lifted it off the crumpled bed for a moment, then let it fall.

Flowers and vanilla. The hint of her scent rising spun him right back to last night, the seamless pleasure continuation he'd thought was a given, blown to pieces by one arm-waving Mayor.

His phone vibrated in his pocket, and he pulled it out.

Damn. It was Cassie. The last thing he needed right now, still he might as well get it over.

'Morning Ed, didn't I tell you the Chateau was a bad idea? I hear you've been rumbled!' Her disgustingly smug note made his guts squirm.

How the hell did she know so soon? He wasn't going to give her the satisfaction of asking, but her bright morning voice made him want to strangle her.

'Hey! Whatever!' He aimed for an easy, don't-give-a-damn response, even though his stomach sagged at the thought of starting the challenge from scratch again. 'Can't win 'em all.'

'So I expect your stripper's all over you like a rash now she knows what you're worth?' Cassie made no attempt to hide her gloating purr.

Something in that attack made his neck prickle. 'Millie's not a stripper, and if you must know, she's stormed off because the last thing she wants is a rich guy. She's leaving.'

'Really?' Cassie's gloat turned sharply to inquisition, then softened to apology. 'Mother's very contrite for blowing your cover you know.'

'Sorry?'

'When she crashed into the cottage earlier – she had no idea you were entertaining a woman. She's been on the phone ever since, ecstatic, pretty much got you married off already.'

So that explained Cassie's call. The rest he could imagine, but strange that Millie hadn't said anything.

'Well, I guess it's game-over this time. Fine by me, respite is well overdue.' He made himself sound way more enthusiastic than he felt. 'A good bout of field-playing is in order, before I settle down for Attempt Two!'

What the hell was wrong with him? He'd usually be whooping at the thought.

'Not so fast.' Cassie's words were measured enough for him to hear her brain ticking. Never a good sign. 'I don't see why we can't change the rules here. This whole challenge has been a walk in the park for you this far, given your date was wanting a low-cost guy. Why don't we carry on? A stripper who hates money has to be the ultimate test now she knows about your cash.'

'For the last time, Cassie, she's not a...'

But Cassie was talking over him. 'So carry on where you left off, and see if you can take it to the end.' And she was sounding exuberant now. 'Only this time it's going to be really hard.'

He dragged in a breath as he snapped his phone shut.

Hard? His thoughts slid back to Millie, as she'd stormed away from breakfast.

Impossible more like.

**

Two hours would be good, he'd thought, for cooling off time.

Or maybe one hour thirty. Whilst he caught up on some work. Sorted.

But the work wasn't working out, and there was only so much pacing a guy could do, and forty minutes later he was quartering the village, scouring every heaving cafe-bar for that haystack hair. Bad luck for him there was a Sunday morning market. How the hell he was going to find her, when the whole of Provence had descended to clog the streets, was beyond him. Fifteen minutes flashed past, then thirty. By now she could easily be back at the

Chateau, might even have left.

His chest constricted at the thought. New plan. He needed to head back, and fast. That way he might have a chance of catching her before she went. Breaking into a run, he careered across the village square, colliding with tourists, ignoring the incensed cries that echoed after him. Reaching the grassy space at the edge of the buildings, he paused in the dappled shade of the plane trees, catching his breath, taking one last look, just in case.

Boots. His heart gave a bang. Sticking out from behind a tree. 'Millie?'

He dashed around, and found her, back propped against the trunk, legs stretched out in the dust. Head lolling, hair like she'd been dragged through a hedge, as per usual, a half-eaten French stick in her lap.

Fast asleep.

Full lips just begging for a Sleeping Beauty kiss. Or maybe not, if he valued his life, given the smoke that had been coming out of her ears as she left. Crouching beside her, he rested his hand in soft the crook of her arm and nudged her gently.

'Millie, wake up.'

A snort, a cough, two blinks, and she was staring him straight in the eye.

'I'm not asleep.'

And grouchy as expected.

'Whatever.'

She sniffed, and rumpled her hair, as if that was possible, then she screwed the top off a coke bottle in her hand, took a swig, then pushed it towards him. 'Drink?'

But why wasn't she yelling at him? He shook his head. Pushed away how mussed and sexy she looked as he slid down beside her. 'Okay if I sit down?'

She snorted again, and threw him a sideways dead-eye. Not

114

happy then. That he could live with.

'I see you bought breakfast.' One inane, paltry attempt at polite conversation. He should be able to do better than that.

'My last three Euros. I came to get cash to leave, but there's a block on my card.' She let out a long, disgruntled sigh, picked up a handful of pebbles, and then trickled them to the ground, one by one. 'Looks like I'm stranded. I may yet have to turn to the stripping that you're so fixated with.'

So 'stranded' explained everything, especially the deflation. She wasn't in a strong position. Nice side swipe about the stripping though. Catching an end-on view of her bitter grimace, he sent a personal thank-you to the god of ATM's. Without that card block she'd have been long gone.

'Don't worry, I brought you here, I'll get you home. You can go where you want, when you want.' Not exactly picking-up-the-action-where-they-left-off he'd planned, but he owed her some respect. And he had no idea where the hell the Challenge had disappeared to, or where the need to gush apology was coming from. 'And I'm sorry about the wealth thing. Obviously I didn't know it was so important to you.'

She was staring intently at her feet now, as she drew her knees towards her. 'So why the deception then?'

Why the heck did she have to be wearing shorts? He concentrated on not reaching out to slide his palm along the bronzed sheen of her thigh.

'It's easier not to flaunt the size of my bank balance, that's all. It's not exactly deception.' Hey ho. Another whopper in the making. 'People react differently if they think you've got money.' At least that last bit was true.

'People, as in women?' She studied him through narrowed eyes.

Screwing him down again.

'You could say that, yep.'

'You mean girlfriends?'

'No, not girlfriends Millie! I do pleasure, not girlfriends, remember?'

One dismissive sniff suggested she was buying it, grudgingly.

'I'd still rather get home by myself than accept your help.'

'I'm sure you would.' Inspiration was seeping through here. 'So why not stay, and go home as planned? That way you stay independent. It's only another day after all.'

She jutted her chin. 'I'm not sure.'

Indecision. Something he had to capitalise on, because the idea of her not staying was suddenly inconceivable. And, hey, it might help if he ignored the way her vest was doing such a bad job of concealing her breasts. This was no time to think about diving in and tonguing those strawberry nipples to distraction.

He cleared his throat, examined the backs of his fingers intently.

'You may be wrong, giving everyone rich a hard time on the basis of one rogue guy in your past. The real problem with your ex wasn't his cash, it was his morals. He'd have been low-life regardless of whether he had money or not. I may be rich, but at least I'm honest, and I'm not claiming to be anything other than I am. It shouldn't matter a jot if I'm loaded or not when all we're doing here is having a fun weekend.'

'Maybe. When you put it like that.'

Great. So long as he could stop obsessing about slipping his hand up the leg of her shorts, stop visualising burying his fingers in her slippery warmth, he was going to keep to his word.

'Don't over-think things. Just enjoy.' He dared a half grin. 'You have to admit last night was great?'

Her face fell. Damn. He should have known that was a bridge too far.

'Yes. But I can't do any more of that if I stay. It's all too...' She hesitated, screwing up her eyes as she searched for the word.

116

'...explosive?'

'That's one word for it.' He couldn't help swinging into a full grin now.

'Are you okay with that?'

How about no? How about hard-on of the decade, banging for release? How about it being absolutely frigging impossible to keep his hands off her for an hour, let alone the rest of the weekend? 'Fine. Whatever makes you comfortable.'

He sprang to his feet. Jeez, he'd have to have some sort of diversion. 'So how about I make you an early lunch? And we'll go and buy some strawberries from the market.'

Mind still on strawberries then.

'Sounds good.' She grasped his out-stretched hand, let him haul her to her feet, before she turned. 'You know this doesn't stop me being cross?'

Cross he could work with. Nothing so new about that.

She dusted down her bottom, and suddenly she was dead-eyeing him again.

What now?

'And one more thing – about my boxes...'

Who gave a damn about boxes anyway? A flicker of unease passed over her face. He'd instantly regretted lashing out about them back there anyway.

She had him fixed now with a fierce glare. 'I need you to know, I'm not ripping *anybody* off.'

∗∗∗

Distance.

Ed decided distance was definitely the key to success here. It should be possible to whip up a passable lunch, and keep his hands of her, so long as she didn't come too close. If he could keep her at bay he'd be A-okay. Which was why he'd positioned her up on a bar stool, half way down the room, hulling strawberries. Except Millie, being Millie, was never going to make things easy, and right now she was sliding down to the floor, arching herself achingly towards him.

'Where are you going now?' He struggled to sound chilled.

'Just to look at that photo over there. I noticed it before, but that was before your Mayor spilled his beans, so I didn't realise it was your family then. That's if you don't mind?'

He aimed for unconcerned. 'No, that's fine.'

Except it was anything but. Millie knowing this was his home changed everything – and not in a good way. The first woman to have gained access to his inner world was dangerous enough to bring him out in a prickling sweat. But on the other hand, anything that kept her the other side of the kitchen was a plus for him. He tore himself away from the view of her perfect ass sashaying in the opposite direction, and went in search of eggs instead, dragging the back of his hand across his forehead to scrape away the perspiration.

'Boy, I can pick you out right away. You must've been born moody and rock jawed. So come and show me who everyone else is.'

That darned photo. They were heading for a train wreck.

'Well, my parents should be obvious, I'm the dark one you already spotted, Cassie's the smallest one, Finn and Sophie are the big ones.'

'And everyone blond except for you.'

So she'd noticed. It would've been more remarkable if she hadn't. He braced himself for the explanation. 'That's because I'm adopted.'

He watched the airy expression drop off her face. Why the hell had he bothered to spill that one now? It was hardly necessary.

118

He could easily have fudged it, and maybe he would have done if he hadn't been wanting to retaliate, not for the way she'd crashed through his privacy barriers, but for the way she was opting out of sex. Pain for pain. She was making him damned uncomfortable. He could do the same for her.

'Ah...' She floundered, but only for a moment, then she collected herself and flicked him a small smile. 'Well you all look very happy anyway. And in a way being adopted is special, it's like you've been chosen.'

He let out a derisive snort.

'Everyone always smiles for the camera.' Best set her straight about that, before he lobbed in the next bit. 'And I wasn't exactly chosen. There's another sister too who's older. She's not there, but she's my mother.'

'Right...' She rubbed her nose pensively. 'I see...'

Except she didn't. She had no idea what it was like to be the cuckoo in the happy family nest, to be the one whose mother had walked away and not come back. How would she? He was cracking through the eggs now, smashing them on the worktop edge, and then flinging them into a bowl. Hammering them to a froth with the whisk.

'She got pregnant on holiday in Italy when she was seventeen, way too young to settle down obviously, so my grandparents adopted me, and brought me up like I was theirs. They were still young when it happened, and they had Cassie afterwards, just to make things really cosy.'

Seemingly oblivious to his bitter aside, she ran a slow finger across the glass.

'And what about your real dad?'

How like Millie not to leave it at that.

With a crash, he grabbed a pan, and threw it onto the hob to heat. 'An Italian mountain guide. We never met – he was killed in

119

a climbing accident when I was small. You could say he's responsible for my dark hair and not much else, apart from the name Eduardo, and my bad temper of course.' One more crash, as if to emphasise the last bit.

'Eduardo. That's cool.' Along the kitchen Millie put back the photo, and drew in a long breath, before she returned, and grasped the glass bowl.

'Great! So that's the strawberries done.'

Well done Millie. Nice change of subject. And his dirty laundry hung out for the world to see. Messy or what? He grimaced at the strewn pile of strawberry stalks she'd left, bleeding across the work surface. The first time he'd let a woman into his domain, and she'd cut straight into his underbelly with one easy slice. Exactly why he'd always kept them well away. 'Damn, way too hot!' The eggs spat savagely as they hit the smoking oil.

And damn for the way he'd been riled enough to let all that out. It was like he was sixteen again, and all he wanted to do was kick the hell out of something, and the only thing that ever helped was to blow something up. Why the heck hadn't he simply emptied the ATM earlier himself, sent her on her way, and avoided all this?

But she was here, and she was responsible for unleashing all those old feelings. And she had it in her power to offer him explosions ten times more effective than rock-face blasting.

He'd just have to make damned sure she came through on that one.

CHAPTER TEN

OMELETTE, albeit slightly over-browned, delicious smoked salmon and salad, followed by strawberries and thick cream, was helping Millie ease back into the land of the living. She extended a tentative hand for more chilled white. She'd been hungry, and way too busy eating to talk, whilst Ed, on the other hand, had maintained a silence of the brooding kind. And the downside to that was his moody scowl, which made him ten times less available, yet ten times hotter at the same time, if that was even possible.

She mustn't let her guard too far down. However well Ed cooked, he was a lot less real and honest than she had thought, whatever his excuses to the contrary, although it was impossible to focus on his dishonesty without her own conscience niggling. It wasn't as if he'd asked, and it wasn't that she'd deceived, but she hadn't gone out of her way to make him aware of the truth of where she came from either. And earlier on this morning she'd been healthily furious with him, cross enough to storm across the village and attempt to make her escape. But two things were nagging at her now. One, the way she'd been so easily persuaded to stay, despite the fact he'd offered her an immediate free passage out of town, and two, the way her earlier fuming had subsided, way too quickly.

'One refill.' He topped her up, without meeting her eye, and clunked the bottle down into the ice bucket, those dangerous lips of his ironed into one grim line.

'Thanks.' She tried a grimace of a smile which she suspected he even didn't see, let alone try to return. They could go on like this all day. Or she could lob in a question and try to see where the trouble lay.

'So did you see much of your real mum when you were growing up?'

Bull's eye! That brought his head jerking to attention. Hitting the nerve, then instantly regretting it as she read the storm in his eyes.

'As if.' A disparaging snarl shot through his scowl. 'She was at Oxford, then when I was two she went to America on a uni exchange, and she stayed out there, pursuing a glittering academic career. Thirty odd years on, she's approximately two steps away from running the world, not that I'd know particularly, because we're what's technically known as estranged.'

'You sound cynical.' Putting it mildly.

'Nope, it was her life, she made her choices. It's nothing to me.' Tipping back in his chair now, he fixed her with a stare bleak enough to chill her blood.

Somehow she couldn't believe they had no relationship at all. 'And you don't ever catch up now?'

'You are joking? Why might I want to do that? I only have contempt for someone who dumped me and ran.'

Any hope in Millie's voice leached away. 'You sound as if you hate her?'

'I wouldn't give anyone so low-grade the benefit of such strong emotion.'

'Aren't you judging too harshly?' She studied him, working out exactly how far she could go here, knowing her chin was jutting too defiantly. 'From where I stand, your mother made a damned brave choice when she opted to have you. I mean, having a baby at seventeen must have taken guts.'

The dark rims of his eyelids flashed as he rounded on her. 'So what do you know?'

She dragged in a breath. No way could she let him know the truth. That she knew exactly what his mother had gone through.

'Not much.' Up to her neck, sinking fast, but still fighting, knowing she had to say her piece. 'Enough to know that having a child isn't an easy option, nor is giving it up. It probably ripped her heart out.'

His hollow sneer bounced off the empty plates. 'Don't tell me, that's why she threw herself into her work?'

'However much you trust the people you left the child with, I'm guessing you'd have to block out the pain somehow.'

'How come you're suddenly the expert?' He rounded on her accusingly.

Oh hell, damage limitation needed, urgently. She so shouldn't have gone here. What the heck had made her wade in, and end up drowning in trouble? Why had she opened herself up for this?

'Believe me, I'm simply talking as an outsider, offering a fresh view, a woman's perspective.' Locking eyes with him, to be sure she'd made her position clear, she guessed he'd bought it. 'But did you ever talk to her about it?'

'She was never around to ask.'

She'd take that as a no then. How the hell had they got here? Blowing out a long sigh, Millie pushed her hair up off her forehead, trying hard to hide the OMG moment she was having, behind her hand. Here was one guy about thirty odd years old, terrified of commitment, still raw as red meat because his mother left him. It didn't take a genius to make the connection.

'Well if you do ever get around to asking her, you may find you get a new insight.' Enough said. Time to run. She pushed back her chair and stood up. 'But right now, I'm going to clear theses plates.'

***

Millie, face down on a sun lounger by the pool later that afternoon, wriggled to pull the sweat dampened vest away from her itching back, and focused on the cola-stained ice cubes melting in the glass beside her. If she screwed up her eyes, she could make out Ed on the next lounger, face like a thunder cloud, head bent over his laptop. Might as well have had *KEEP OUT* tattooed on his forehead.

So much for a fun weekend.

That promise had gone downhill at break-neck speed and disappeared from view. At least when he was wrapped in his high-security barrier of fierce concentration, there was less danger of temptation. Because earlier, somewhere amongst him sweeping the strawberry leaves off the worktop with those broad, strong hands of his, crashing at the sink as he rinsed out the wine bottle, and tossing the dirty plates into the dishwasher, her insides had started to melt, despite all efforts to keep her libido firmly in the ice age. By the time they came outside, she was fighting a full-scale desire inferno, which she could only put down to the white wine at lunch. And possibly the light-shaft glimpse of raw, vulnerable man. Who'd have thought that one tiny crack in that rough, tough exterior could be so impossibly sexy? The thought of it made her heart squish, and beat in the weirdest kind of way.

Sexy? Impossibly sexy?

She needed to get a grip. Torched by the guy she was determined to keep at arm's length was no way a good look, especially when he'd given her every reason to despise him. And darn that she'd thought to bring every item of clothing except a bikini! She gave her vest another tug, to be sure it was covering her lacey shorts, and brushed a trickle of sweat out of her eye. Where the hell had this sudden modesty come from? Deep down she knew covering up was the only way for her to be when confronted with his burning sexuality. What happened to the easy, confident woman, who taught her pupils to work what they had to the max, the one who, in her other life might have been strolling up and down the poolside, in control, working her moves just for herself? That girl had shrunk away, hiding in the face of the physical attraction onslaught that was Ed Mitchum, because when there was a detonator like him in the midst, her survival instinct had kicked in. She knew she'd be safer dressed in a nun's habit, and trussed in a chastity belt with a hundred locks. When Ed was around there was no need to work anything. Her body was doing that, and spontaneously combusting all by itself.

And swimming was the last thing she'd planned on doing in a vest, but maybe she was going to have to make a dash for the water after all. It was either that or expire.

'Think I may just have a dip.' Easing to sitting, her brain momentarily dizzied by the heat, distantly aware of Ed easing upright, laptop forgotten, every atom of his concentration locked on to her now. The stones hot under her feet as she tiptoed, and folded onto the pool edge, trying to ignore the way his gaze set her already burning skin on fire. Trailing a finger into the water, daring to turn half an eye towards him, knowing she needed to keep him in her sights, like a watchful cat asleep with one eye open, just in case.

Just in case what?

That slip of a smile that left all on its own before she could put the brakes on it, colliding with Ed. Then the slightest twitch of his lips, the infinitesimal creasing at the corners of his eyes that sent her stomach plummeting to the pool bottom. No choice but to follow it. She slid off the poolside, and let the silky depths engulf her, scraping the water out of her eyes as she surfaced.

'Deliciously cool.' Pushing back her dripping hair strands, finding her gaze dragged inextricably towards him. And damn to the way the chill of the water had failed to lower her lust temperature.

'Maybe I'll join you.' He eased forward lazily.

Oh no! That had to be the last thing she wanted! 'Aren't you working?'

'Slight problem, given that something appears to be ejecting my laptop' He shot her a smoldering grin, and in one swoop his laptop was on the floor and he'd sprung into a horizontal dive, and hit the water. And he was heading straight for her.

'Whoa!' She backed away from the splash, instinctively trying to save herself. Damn. Too little, too late. She gasped as his body crashed into hers. Another second, and he captured her mouth with the force of a tidal wave, kissing her, full and rough and hard, snatching away her breath and her resistance in one easy move. As her legs gave way, she dissolved against the slick muscular planes of his body, watching the azure flashes of the pool, blurry through half closed eyes. Pulling her vision into focus, the close-up view of his eyelashes, clumped and wet, sent her banging heart into overdrive, and filled her body with a new, and urgent strength. Now, when his erection drove into her belly, she forged against it, carried along by the desperate ache that pulsed through her core, and pooled like burning fudge between her legs.

She really shouldn't be.

Mumbling through the kiss. 'I really shouldn't be...'

'What?' His voice husky against her face as he broke away.

'This...'

'We both know you want to...' And then he was kissing her again, but harder, his hands slipping around her waist, guiding and lifting, as, buoyed by the water, she rose, and wrapped her thighs tight around his waist, flattening the heat of her need against the thrust of his stomach. Her insides turning to molten gold as he drew back her shorts and slicked a finger deep inside her.

126

'Oh!'

And then another.

'Oh, yes!' Locking her ankles tighter as she writhed on his hand, her own mews echoed by the deep growls that caught in his throat, as his erection drilled against her ass.

This was so not in the plan for this afternoon. So not in the plan ever again. Her eyes wide open now, and not seeing a thing. But knowing that the delicious blunt tip of him was nudging, pushing, finding a way, and she was dizzyingly, amazingly ready to take the whole driving length of him.

'No, we need...' How had they got this far without protection?

'Yes...' His affirmation was more of a groan.

And he wasn't even listening. 'Ed! What about a condom?'

One abrupt jive, and he'd pulled away. 'Damn, sorry! I'll sort it.' Then he was out, drenching the poolside, hurrying towards the cottage, hopping as his bare feet hit the gravel path, and she was left, head spinning, gasping for breath.

Oh my! Okay. Try to focus on the wiggly lines of the mosaic tiles through the water. *Try to stop your heart banging like a wave machine, get your butt into gear, and get yourself out of this one!* Because more sex with Ed was such a bad idea. Always had been. Getting out of the water had to be a step in the right direction. And kicking herself, hard, for what just happened may be no bad idea either.

By the time Ed skidded back onto the pool terrace, she was swathed in a towel, leaning forwards, patting her hair dry, and working on a tangle.

'What the..? I thought we..?' His brow furrowed, and his eyes narrowed.

'I'm sorry, I got carried away back there.' Breathlessly, she fought to keep her voice even and tried to avoid his gaze, as his expression morphed from incomprehension, to disbelief. 'It's better if we don't.'

Not wanting to be mean, not meaning to mess anyone around, but it was a matter of self preservation. When he touched her she lost all sense of control, all sense of everything. Not a good place to be.

'Better for who exactly?' His sniff of disgust could have come from a raging bull.

At least he was easier to resist when he was fuming. But then he reached out, grasped her arm raggedly, screwed his head round to fix her with a penetrating stare, and a giveaway shiver zipped up her spine. And down again. Damn her treacherous body! Damn the way the smallest touch of his hand had her in pieces. Filling her lungs with oxygen, she tried to be honest.

'Like I said this morning...' *And how long ago that seemed.* 'I just can't handle it.'

If she stuck her chin in the air, he'd know she meant it, though judging by the stormy darkening of his eyes, he'd already got the message loud and clear. She just wished her own body would accept her final word on it too.

'And as *I* said this morning, it's your loss.' He spoke with a curl of his lip, as he let her wrist drop, his chocolate voice strangely harsh and flinty 'but if my plans for this evening are out the window that leaves us free to attend the Reception at the Chateau. My mother will be delighted. I hear you two have already met, by the way.'

'Er...' *Oh, shucks!* Opening and closing her mouth like an idiot. Not attractive. She shrunk under his accusing stare. What the heck happened to easy-going Ed?

'An evening in my mother's company or a pleasure max? I know which I'd choose.' He gave a derisory sneer.

'A Reception sounds great, thanks.'

People. Company. Safety. All good. At this moment a trip to the gallows would have sounded less dangerous than a pleasure max with Ed.

'Have it your own way, as usual.' He gave a hollow laugh, as he slung a towel around his waist, swiped his wet hair off his forehead with his wrist, grabbed his laptop and backed away across the terrace. 'I'll leave you to it then! Be ready for seven. And I may as well warn you, my mother is very exacting!'

***

Ed grimaced at his reflection in the hall mirror, gave his tie a final yank into position, and blocked the iron hand of dread that closed around his entrails. Tonight had barely started, but it was already looking like a very bad idea. He snorted as he took in the unfamiliar dark hollows under his eyes, snorted again as he remembered the reason for them.

One weekend with Millie, not yet done, and already it was a train-wreck.

Which only went to prove how right he'd been all along. If this challenge had taught him one thing it was that his women-at-a-distance approach was the only way for him to be. Ed Mitchum, with a woman at close quarters, equaled one short cut to disaster. Look at him now. Haggard, bad tempered, frustrated as hell, beyond ready to explode. This afternoon he'd almost had sex without protection, which for a guy like him was tantamount to financial suicide, given the paternity suits that could ensue. What *had* he been thinking? What's more, thanks to Millie and her damned probing, he'd spilled his guts about his adoption, and opened yet another festering can of worms. Sure he thrived on competition, yes, he was driven to succeed, but could he justify putting himself through mayhem like this simply to win some stupid challenge? Right now he'd happily throw a street of houses in Edinburgh at Will and Cassie if it meant getting out of it.

Somewhere along the line, he wasn't quite sure where, Millie had tipped his life upside down. And her whisking away any sexual enjoyment he may have wrung out of the situation by way of compensation, was the final wave of the finger from her. So tonight was set to stir things on a lot of levels.

He always failed to please his mother. It was worth breaking his lifelong refusal to appear with a plus one, if only to see the look on his mother's face when he walked in with someone as unsuitable as Millie. Millie's Cinderella look was guaranteed to throw his mother into a blue fit. Perfect payback for her planning to marry him off.

As for Millie, dropping a woman like her into one of his mother's soirees had to be like throwing her to the wolves. To hell with it, he thought, as he felt one more knot add itself to his already twisted gut. Millie's had every opportunity to choose a much better option for both of them, but she'd refused.

'Hey, someone scrubs up well.'

Her voice lilting down the hall, and the click-clack of heels, caught him off guard.

Damn. Ten minutes early too. Bracing himself for another shredded outfit, he spun to face her.

'Wow!' Picking his jaw off the floor would be an understatement. For a second the power of further speech was whooshed away.

'What? I don't look that bad do I?' She hesitated, stopping a few feet away, yet close enough for her delicious warm scent to reach him.

He dragged in a breath of her. Something about the dismayed furrows crinkling her brow sent his stomach into free-fall. Compliments needed, and urgently.

'Bad? No, absolutely not. Different...' Struggling, he shot her a grin he hoped would take her mind off his gawping, as he drank in the way her streamlined dress clung in all the right places. 'Stunning, amazing...'

Heart stoppingly so. Knowing whatever he said no way covered the perfection of those vertiginous heels accentuating the curves of her calves, or the way her hair, swept upwards, caught in a series of waves, not a hay-wisp in sight, revealed the aching vulnerability of her neck. How the immediate urge to sink his teeth into the pale skin at the base of her collarbone was almost overpowering. He cleared his throat, caught the mocking grin that was scything his way.

'No need to look quite so gob-smacked. I can do smart when it's called for, I've got a French grandmother, remember?' She pushed an escaping strand of fringe out of her eye. 'She taught me never to travel without a little black dress. This might only be a lycra version but it does the trick. And my whale-net tights mean I don't completely bow to convention.'

'Whale net? So that would be fishnet on a grand scale?' And a thousand times more sexy by the looks of it. His grin of appreciation had escaped before he could stop it. 'And so pleased you're holding out to be different.' Not that he could imagine she would ever conform.

'So shall we going then?' She was already past him, one hand on the door handle.

'If you're sure you're ready. There's still time to change your mind — opt for the alternative?' Raising an eyebrow, knowing he was on a loser here, but not able to resist the tease.

'Nice try. You already know the answer to that.' She rolled her eyes. *Was that a smile she was stifling?* 'You look pretty awesome yourself, by the way, for someone who spends so much time in a quarry, and dates according to The Big Bang Theory.'

'Meaning?'

'One explosion and you move onto the next woman. Fitting

somehow, given your occupation.'

Without waiting for a retort, she was off across the court-yard, hips swaying delectably with every long, determined stride. *Awesome!* He paused momentarily to take in the view, but at the rate she was going, if he didn't get moving she'd soon be a speck on the horizon. Tackling her about her Big Bang jibe would have to wait.

'Hang on speedy! There's no rush!' His arm inadvertently brushing against her as he arrived at her side, was answered with a jerk as she jolted away.

What the..?

'We might as well get there, no point hanging round, and I'm perfectly capable of walking in heels without help, thanks all the same.' She shot him a withering scowl.

'Whatever.' He stepped away, biting back a smile as he noted the no-go zone clearly delineated by her rigid sticky-out arms. 'Walking at the required distance here?'

She answered that with a silent sneer that merged into another eye roll.

Point taken, but no way was she going to be able to stand unaided in *those* heels at the Chateau entrance. He held in his amusement, counting down as they made their way alongside the monumental walls, her heels clacking with every stomping step, round the last corner and, Bingo! – the fine gravel path gave way to a sea of polished cobbles, and she was left teetering at the shore edge, arms flapping as she struggled to balance.

He flinched as her growl of pure displeasure rolled up off the stones, and zinged straight to his nether regions. *Wham. Direct hit.*

'Okay Mitchum, you win. I may need to hang on to you, but you can stop that gloating right now!' She flashed him a searing glare, which bounced right off, then moved on airily. 'Hey, that's one cool portcullis you have here.'

Nice change of subject to cover her climb-down.

He flung a nonchalant arm around her, caught her waist in the crook of his elbow, thrown off by the way the huge entrance hadn't fazed her one bit. No trace of the expected nerves or jitters in the fingers that snuck under his jacket, clamped onto his hip. There was no way any of this was over-awing her. If anyone was suffering here, it was him, and as they progressed further into the lofty entrance hall, his inner alarm bells began to clang. And now, as they were approaching the high doorway of the party room, and could hear the elegant murmuring of the guests, his mental alarms were deafening. Okay, this was only some measly reception his mother had organised, but it was the first time he had walked into any social event with a plus-one. And worse, due to the unfortunate combination of heel height and flooring materials, they were going to be making their entrance in an unmistakably public clinch. So where along the line exactly, had his indisputable Single-guy Survival rules become toast?

'I hope you're ready for this?' The scent of Millie's hair blurred his vision as he hissed in her ear as they approached the megalithic, partly-open door.

'You bet I am, bring it on.' Her sparky laughter faded to concern as her eyes met his, and her free hand crossed his body and arrived, uninvited, on his wrist. 'Hey, are you sure you're ok with this?'

'Never better.' Lying through his teeth, he pulled his hand away to readjust the knot of his tie, and swallowed to relieve a mouth as dry as Arizona. And how come she was so at ease anyway? He'd expected her to be at least a little over-awed by the spectacular surroundings.

'So am I wrong to be picking up tension vibes here?' She twitched her mouth sideways, drilling him with her best screw-the man-down stare.

Why the hell did she have to complicate every little thing?

'You may as well know, my older brother, Finn, is the golden boy in this family. I've never yet done anything yet to please my mother, and I'm unlikely to break that tradition this evening.' He gave a dismissive snort. 'I'm firmly cast in the role of the black sheep, and I've never yet failed to live up to expectations.'

And why the hell did he crack and spill his guts every time?

Her brow furrowed as her eyes snagged on his clenched fists below his suit cuffs. No doubt she'd clocked the white of his knuckles, because she put one palm, flat on his lapel.

'Don't worry.' Her cheek nestled close to his chest as her low words brushed his ear. 'We'll have one glass of fizz, and if there's any trouble we'll run, okay?'

She was patting him soothingly now, chin tilted upwards, eyes all smokey with reassurance. So not how he'd planned it. So darn back-to-front, upside-down, messed up. So darned Millie Brown.

'Whatever. It's cool. I can handle it.'

'I know you can.' Extracting her arm from inside his jacket, she snaked it through his elbow and squeezed. 'So if you're breathing again, perhaps we should go in?'

CHAPTER ELEVEN

'WOW! Spectacular chandeliers!' Millie blinked as they slid into the room, momentarily dazzled by the glittering cascades suspended high above them, and eased her grip on Ed's arm as she stepped off polished boards onto the safety of a carpet. 'But best of all, a floor I can stand up on.'

'First things first.' One raised eyebrow and Ed was back in control, a waiter was there, and a glass of champagne was pressed into her hand. 'Have a swig, and I'll introduce you to the old lady. Then we can get away from all these yawnsville guests and have a wander onto the terrace – the view from there is amazing.'

Secluded was exactly what she didn't want.

'Aren't we going to mingle? I love parties like this, you meet the most unexpected people.'

'Mingle?' He cocked his head at her, with a puzzled frown. 'You sound like you go to receptions on a daily basis?'

'Errrr. Not so much now.' Damn. Too much information. Her parents' parties, their moneyed guests, her privileged past, everything she had strived to get away from, and one game she couldn't give away. She flailed for a diversion. 'Hey, your Mother's over there. Is now a good time to say 'Hi'?'

'Good idea. I must say, you're very chilled with all this.'

Not exactly how she'd describe herself, as his steering hand arrived in the small of her back, and set her heart thrashing. She flashed him a smile as they sidled across the room, making their way past small groups of guests. 'Mothers are cool, I love meeting them.'

He was practically edible in a suit. She so hadn't bargained for melting like this when she brushed up against his lapel. Dammit. She'd decided she couldn't handle getting physical with him, but now she was having all these thoughts right in front of his Mum.

As Ed whooshed her up to his Mother, and stepped back himself, Millie returned the welcoming smile of the woman from the kitchen, and prayed her cheeks weren't as pink as they felt.

'Mother, this is Millie.' Ed's lip curled, and his brows knitted.

'Thanks Eddie, but we've already met haven't we Millie?' Mrs Mitchum rose above Ed's stroppy toddler act. 'Lovely to see you again.'

'Hello Mrs Mitchum.' Millie extended her hand.

'Please – call me Frances.'

Millie narrowed her eyes at Ed, who, hands in pockets, was rolling his eyes behind his mother's shoulder. Side by side he and his adopted mother were strikingly different, yet with similarities around their eyes.

'You know, I thought I recognised you this morning Millie.' Mrs Mitchum still holding Millie's hand, took a small step back as she surveyed her. 'You're Amelia, aren't you? Helen Brunswick-Brown's daughter? I've seen you in London at the hospital fund raisers. Your Mother and I are on the same committees.'

'Oh, right. Er, possibly. Oh, probably.' Millie's stomach crashed down, and puddled somewhere near her stilettos. So not what she wanted to hear.

'Aren't you the one who makes the boxes?'

'Er, actually, yes, that's me.' Millie ignored Ed's eyebrows, shooting somewhere beyond the ceiling, fought her own heart trying to escape through her throat.

'Beautiful boxes, I have one in my study here.' Frances, smiling widely at Millie, sniffed as she turned. 'Eddie, will you go and get me a drink please, and make sure not to come straight back, Millie and I can't possibly chat with you standing there, gawping.'

Millie swallowed hard as she reclaimed her hand, hoping the immediate danger of depositing her lunch on the carpet had passed, and watched Ed's back, disappearing in the sea of other dark suits. At least he was out of the way, temporarily.

'So, Millie, tell me how your family are getting on...'

In a blur, Millie bumbled through the next ten minutes. The chat was easy, keeping a vigilant watch for Ed's return was harder, and when it happened she missed it.

'Hey, you two are getting on well.' He was already at her shoulder, his breath hot on her neck, handing his Mother a drink, and his tone was caustic.

'Don't take any notice of him, Millie, he's only teasing.' Frances's beatific beam transformed to a grimace, with accompanying eye roll. 'Millie and I have lots to talk about, Eddie.'

'I'm sure you do.'

'Yes, we've been catching up, it's been great.' Millie kept her voice light. No way could she deal with the fall-out with Ed, in front of his Mother. Delaying tactics called for. 'But if you'll excuse me a moment, I need to go to the bathroom.'

One place Ed wouldn't follow her. At least there she could re-group, decide what to do.

***

'You've made us wait a long time for today Eddie, but it's been worth it. Millie's lovely, a wonderful choice. Well done.'

Ed, eyes glued to Millie's rear view, winding across the room, measured the depth of his mothers purr, and decided protest was pointless. She'd find out the truth soon enough.

'You didn't spot her tattoo then?' No harm in telling it like it is, just to be bad.

'Her tattoo?' His mother took a sip of her champagne, eyeing him levelly across the top of her glass. 'Of course I saw her tattoo. I could hardly miss it. And? '

'And it didn't put you off?'

'Oh, don't be so old fashioned Eddie, everyone has tattoos these days, it would be more surprising if an artistic girl like her didn't, and it was very tasteful. Even some of my friends from the health club have...'

'Okay, hold it, too much information.' And damn to how he'd misread his mother.

So much for an upside down day.

'She's perfect for you. I always worried you wouldn't find anyone from the same background who would interest you, and that's so important. The family are Knightsbridge based, her father's something big in the chemical industry, but then you'll know that.'

'No, er, yes, er, obviously.' He took a large slug of his drink.

'Whatever, I'm very pleased you've brought her to meet us.' His mother gave him a quizzical stare, just for a moment, before bashing on. 'And she's obviously exceptionally fond of you.'

He gulped, choked, and narrowly missed spraying his mother full in the face with champagne.

'What?' He gritted his teeth, making every effort not to shout. This was unbelievable. His mother had gone way too far this time. 'And why exactly would you say that?'

'Because of the adoring way she looks at you darling, surely you aren't going to pretend you haven't noticed? When these things happen, you can't fight them.'

He snorted, loudly, as he spun around. 'And you wonder why I come home on my own. Catch you later Mother.'

'Well don't run off before we've organised for you two love-birds to come over for lunch tomorrow!'

No mystery where Cassie got her bossy and domineering streak from, or why he had his parental-avoidance tactics honed.

'Sorry, no chance, we're busy all day.' He scanned the room, trying to locate Millie, so he could check out the 'adoring looks' theory for himself, as soon as. It had to be a figment of his mother's over-active imagination, didn't it? Millie, with her serious man-ban would never have fallen for him. Hot and sexy she may be, but she wasn't stupid, and he couldn't have made his position clearer. His Mother's words echoed round his head. When these things happen, you can't fight them. That surely couldn't be why Millie was backing off from him, could it?

He loosened his tie, undid the top button of his shirt, and ran the back of his hand across his brow, fighting the constriction which was gripping his throat.

Sheesh, it could be, it might be, and it damn well probably was. Thinking about it, her falling for him was the only sensible explanation. How could he have been so blind? She hadn't exactly played straight about her background, not that he was in any position to take her to task on that one, and that deception had suddenly lost all significance in the light of his mother's new revelation. But it did show that she was capable of hiding the truth. If he racked his brains he'd remember Millie's exact excuse for calling a halt with their sex. Something about it being too explosive, and although at the time he'd taken it as a back-handed compliment, he'd been too blown away with annoyance to analyse the reasoning behind it. Okay, his immediate instinct now was to haul her outside and have this out with her, but there was no point in panicking before it was strictly necessary.

A lurch in his stomach alerted him to Millie's return. She'd slipped back into the room, and was immediately accosted by some fearsome old dowager wearing almost as much crystal as the chandeliers. Fascinating to see the way Millie sparkled as she chatted easily and animatedly. Within minutes she was surrounded by a group of fusties, all rapt, and seemingly hanging on her every word, Millie radiant and smiling at the centre, a million miles away from the muddy, blood-stained girl he pulled out of the field. An involuntary rush of pride that she was his gushed through him. *What the heck?* He stamped on that one, and hard. As if she sensed she was being watched, Millie raised her chin to gaze around. His chest twanged as their eyes locked, then a flicker of softness passed across her face that had his heart plummeting and bouncing off the deck.

Despite taking every precaution to make it clear that he was not in the market for caring, she was still looking at him like that. Worse still, he'd have expected the knowledge to douse his out of control libido like a bucket of freezing water, and as yet it definitely hadn't. What was that maddening saying about Mother's always being right? Unbelievable. Millie might have polished up, and she might be wearing a veneer of social confidence he hadn't seen before, but he knew that inside that she was vulnerable, and the last thing in the world he wanted to do was hurt her. So when he did manage to tear Millie away from the canapés and the champagne and the countesses, they had some serious talking to do.

CHAPTER TWELVE

'HEY, that went well, don't you think?' Millie tossed a smile in Ed's direction as they arrived back in the cottage kitchen, knowing how hollow those too-bright words sounded.

Insincere, or another shining example of her glossing over the truth?

She had stretched the evening as far as she could, talking to everyone in sight, for as long as humanly possible. Safety in numbers, surround yourself with a crowd, she'd played every card in the book to avoid being alone with Ed, and having to face the inevitable inquisition about her background, and why she hadn't come clean about it. It served her right for being less than straight, and she knew she had to face the music at some point. As Ed tossed down his jacket and ripped off his tie, she knew now it was completely unavoidable, and she'd rather get it over sooner than later

'How the evening went depends on who you are and where you were standing. At least you and my Mother appeared to be having a ball.' Ed threw two tumblers onto the kitchen island, grappled the top of a whisky bottle, and fixed her with a penetrating stare as he sloshed out two ridiculously large measures and pulled up a stool. 'Take this, sit down, we need to talk.'

Ominous, but expected, and her stomach plummeting like a

stone as she took in the deep furrows on his forehead and eased onto the seat next to his. A smart girl would grab the advantage and get in first. Snatching a hurried breath she launched her defense.

'Yep, about the Amelia thing, I'm a hundred percent sorry, I didn't mean to be misleading but...' Scrutinising his face to gauge his reaction, she realised her nervous babbling was meeting puzzled incomprehension.

'What?' He rubbed a thumb across his eyebrows, distractedly, as if he'd barely heard.

'I'm talking about my Brunswick Brown alter-ego thing? Me not quite being a hundred percent who I actually said I was?'

'Oh that.' He rolled his eyes and gave a dismissive grimace. 'Neither of us has been entirely honest about where we come from, so I guess that makes us even. End of.'

End of? That took the wind right out of her sails.

'Okay.' The thing she'd been stressing over like crazy all evening, he'd dismissed with a shrug. So what the hell did he want to talk about? The stone in her stomach expanded to boulder size. Men never asked to talk, did they? Not if they could possibly avoid it. Not unless they were in the tightest of corners, the rock and a hard place scenario.

'Millie, I've made it clear all along I'm not available haven't I?'

'Yes.' She narrowed her eyes, calculating where the heck he was going with this.

'But I'm worried, because I have reason to believe you're maybe getting too, er...' he hesitated, '...attached.'

Reason to believe? He was talking like a courtroom lawyer here.

'Holding on tight when we were crossing the cobbles on our way back doesn't necessarily mean I'm getting clingy.' True, a night's worth of alcohol had rushed to her erogenous zones with the fresh air, and yes, she had been seriously reconsidering her no-sex decision at that point. Blame the champagne, blame how edible he was wearing a suit, any girl would have been the same. But attachment? That was something else entirely, somewhere she would never go.

'Not clingy. More that perhaps you're falling for me.'

'Excuse me?' She heard herself shriek with incredulity. 'I'm totally not falling for anyone, believe me!'

'Okay, put it another way.' He drew in a long breath. 'Getting too involved perhaps? I'm a pretty attractive package, after all.'

Arrogance like that, and the peppering of anger in her chest exploded.

'And what the hell gave you that idea?' She watched him open his mouth and close it. Obvious then, he wasn't going to tell her what he really thought.

'This and that.' He gave a sheepish shrug. 'Okay, I'll come clean – when you opted out of more sex, I assumed you were pulling back because you were starting to care.'

She bowled him an accusing scowl, watching the bump of his Adam's apple move as he swallowed, and wished it didn't make her tummy turn the way it did.

'Putting two and two together and making five?' She let out what she hoped was a derisory laugh. 'You of all people should know I'd never get involved. The whole point of this weekend is the temporary part.'

Calling a halt because it was too mind-blowing was a whole different story she wasn't going to expand on here, because he'd only twist it around and use it against her. As for caring – she definitely didn't care, did she? The tiniest niggle of doubt needled somewhere deep inside her, but she couldn't, on any level, allow herself to admit that, not even to herself.

'Sure about that?' His dark eyes under even darker brows drilling into her now, turning her insides to hot toffee.

What more assurance did the darned man need, what more

could she give?

'Ed, I came here for fun, I came for the bonk-fest you promised, simply to prove to myself that I could. I already explained that, and you agreed to play the guinea pig, if you remember? I'm sorry to disappoint your huge ego, but you personally have very little to do with it, apart from the obvious bonking bit, obviously.' There, that told him, even if she had said obvious twice. He couldn't ask for more than that, unless... 'Unless you'd like me to sleep with you again, to prove it definitively? Let's have that pleasure max you've been begging for one more time, if that's what you need to know it's fun for me, and nothing more. I prove I can do it one more time. It's neither here nor there for me.'

So, that came out before she'd thought it through, but now it was out there, it was no bad idea. Doing it again could be the best way of proving to herself she didn't give a damn about him, and crepe-suzette to the way her pulse was already racing at the thought. That would be because the man was pure dynamite in the O department, and dammit, she may never get another bite at orgasms like that in the rest of her life. It had to be a now or never kind of a thing, and she'd be stupid not to grab that whilst it was on offer.

He took a deep swig of whisky, and lowered his eyes as he bumped his glass on the table. 'No, I appreciate the offer, but sorry, it's out of the question.'

What? Was Mr Sex-crazed blowing her off? Again. Surely not? 'You are joking?'

'No, it's too big a risk. Great offer, thanks all the same, but count me out of that one.'

Totally infuriating didn't come close. She gritted her teeth and watched his jaw muscle twitch as she tried to work out her next move. When nothing inspirational sprung to mind, she opted instead for a throwaway line. 'Fun whilst it lasted anyway.'

Swirling his whisky round the glass now, he shot her a rueful grin. 'Too bad I'll never get to see those tattoos properly, but I'll have to live with that.'

'What? Now you are being ridiculous, how the heck did you miss my tats?'

'A hundred reasons – your jacket, the dark, the covers, and your vest by the pool. Need I go on?'

'No point backing off all the way and then sounding wistful. It's too late now Mr Mitchum, your loss. Anyway, I think I'll get off to bed. Thanks for a great evening by the way.' She stole one last glance at Ed, brooding over his whisky, tossing her head as she slid to the floor, determined to keep her dignity in place, and the disappointment out of her parting smile.

Pausing for a moment to steady herself before she tackled the walk across the limestone flags, the thought of never holding him again sent a stabbing spasm through her chest. Whoa. Spasms? Never a good look. Then her eye snagged on the iPod dock on the work surface, and suddenly she knew exactly what she had to do. If she took a chance and it went horribly wrong, the worst thing that could happen was that she would end up looking even more desperate and rejected. But what the heck. She had to work fast, seize the moment. Purposefully, she strode across the kitchen, stretched out one quaking finger, and, no idea what was coming, flicked on the music and held her breath.

Great, her luck was in. Lana Del Ray. She recognised it immediately. That smoldering track couldn't be more perfect for what she had in mind, and just to make doubly sure she leaned in and pushed the repeat button. As the opening bars slid across the room Ed's head jerking upwards told her she had surprise on her side too.

***

145

'What the....'

Was that music? Ed let his gaze leave the glass he'd been staring at so fiercely to avoid getting a parting eyeful of Millie's legs as she left. When his eyes snapped back into focus they locked on her across the kitchen. Talk about double takes. He'd heard of OMG moments, and this had to be one. Millie? He wasn't sure what the heck was happening, but man, he wasn't complaining. She had her back to him, legs apart, forcing the split in the back of her skirt open in a way that sent his entire blood supply rushing south, and she was swaying gently in time to the music, smoothing her palms over the curves of that delicious ass as she gyrated her hips. And the melody, all distant harps, and echoing voices singing about bad boys going to heaven, and here was one bad boy who just landed right there himself. Except he wasn't supposed to be doing this.

And then she turned. One twist of her knee, and she was round. And he was picking up his dropped jaw, as she ran her hand around her head, languidly flicking hair clips onto the floor. Shaking and mussing her hair now, slipping him a smooch of a smile before averting her eyes again. So the hayrick was back, but this wasn't a Millie he'd seen before. Sidling now, butt out, working those dynamite curves, pausing to stretch along the work surface, simultaneously smoldering hot, and delectably untouchable. A hundred percent in control. Of him. Of herself. Of the whole damned world if she wanted to be, and he'd happily have licked the ground she walked on whilst she stamped on his tongue with the spike of her stiletto had she asked him.

Shimmying across, she picked up his abandoned tie, and unfurled it with another playful smile, then, eyes lowered again, she let the silky strip slide, drape, caress her curves. Simple. Easy. Aching. Then as she circled, bent, swept her hair across the floor, the most awesome eyeful of cleavage sent his off-the-scale libido rocketing to who knew where. And one scorch of that flash of a smile told him she knew exactly what she was doing to him.

This woman didn't need anyone to save her from anything.

Cross stepping towards him now, one shoulder strap accidentally-on-purpose sliding its way to indecency and racking his erection through the pain threshold. Wiggling her hips, and sending a seismic shudder through him just by slithering the tie across his cheek. Hauling in the scent of her, and knowing this woman was bullet-proof, high incendiary. No way was she going to get hurt. And that knowledge let him right off the guilt hook. He'd have been whooping, but there were other more pressing matters.

'I love that you're going to strip for me.' Growling his appreciation, and not able to resist running a finger up the delicious line of her spine as she paused with her back to him.

And then she was round, her thigh grating over his, her low laugh taunting in his ear. 'This is about lust not sex, it's the tease not the strip – if you want to see what's underneath, you'll have to undress me yourself.'

'Now there's an invitation.' The pyramid of his erection, straining against his suit trousers, cranked up another notch as she lowered her eyes to devour it. 'But two can play at that game, you aren't the only one who can tease...'

'You wouldn't...' She forced her thigh against his shaft, dispatching an unholy volley of pleasure rocketing through his body, as she raised a quizzical eyebrow at him. '...would you?'

Not after that he wouldn't. He might have done, another day, another time, but that nudge pushed him past the point of teasing. Easing to standing, spanning her waist with his hands, one twist and she was on the work surface, dress pushed high, her stocking tops sending his blood-pressure off the scale. Another twist and her knickers were history.

Locking onto the sweetest heat of her mouth, he grazed his

thumb across the thin fabric of her dress. *That had to be the sheerest of bras.* As he found her nipples, pert, and panting for attention she leaned into him with a low moan.

'I'm truly not falling for you Ed, but I do need...' Her voice was bleary as her flickering eyelids.

'Yes..?' Peeling down the strap of her dress, he captured one nipple, an ache throbbing in his groin, as he tugged it between his teeth, then sucked deeply.

'You know the pleasure-max thing...' Her thighs were clamping hot around his hips now, as she thrust onto his stomach, skin silky above her stockings, her bottom sending him into spasm as she rode over the peak of his still-enclosed erection.

'Yes..? He watched her head slip backwards, her lips part as his fingers found her clit. Two fingers and she was clamping on him, her gentle rocking on his hand driving his desire to insane places.

'A pleasure max, like, now would be good...' One husky high-voltage command, encouraging him.

Like now was how it was going to have to be. Thankfully he'd slipped a condom in his pocket.

Unzipping, harder than rock as he rolled on protection, pulling her to meet him, he nudged, edged, pushed, and then he was home, groaning with the pure unadulterated passion. Up to the hilt and plunging, her cries building as he thrust, she was driving him crazy. Her arms grappling around his shoulders, her legs locked around him, her feral groans rising as he drove into her, pushing him higher and higher. And then she was shuddering, hurling back her head, contracting onto him, and then wild, furious, and out of control his own release exploded.

***

'You okay down there?' Burying his face in her hair, he ignored the way the scent of her scalp was already sending new shivers down his spine.

One lazy post-coital clinch, her cheek resting heavy on his chest, and as he pushed back her hair a flash of shoulder and the curve of a bare breast sent another wave juddering down his spine, this time a seismic one. *Damn his libido.* What was it with Millie? Hot sex was supposed to make you satisfied, not desperate for more of the same. Immediately afterwards.

'Sure.' She gave a sniff, disentangled a hand to rub her nose. 'That was great by the way, and the good news is I still don't want to get involved. '

'Pleased to hear it.' He gave a wry grin. 'And the bad news is I still haven't seen your tattoos properly, but maybe we can remedy that? Shall we go to bed?'

Hell of a trite line there, but who cared if it got him where he needed to be.

And bed was a million miles away from his earlier intentions, but he was far from finished here. If anything, he'd barely begun. Disentangling himself, he gave her hand a light tug in the direction of the door.

'It has been a long day.' She let out a sleepy sigh, stretched, but resisted his pull.

'You can say that again.' Hell, it only been this morning that he was scouring the village for her. Although sleep was the last thing on *his* mind now, dammit.

'You sure you can trust me not to fall for you overnight then Mr Irresistible?' Her pout twitched, as if she were biting back a smile. 'We don't want any broken hearts do we?'

Hell, she was mocking him here, big style, and he was taking it. Lapping it up. Right now he'd pretty much take anything she dished out if it meant getting her between the sheets.

'I guess.' One cover-all answer he hoped covered all aspects. Delivered with a dose of hundred watt smile, which slipped out all by itself, nothing to do with him.

That smile never failed to work its magic.

He stood his ground, waited, and raised an eyebrow. *Fast would be good.* Hoping that she wouldn't fix on the ever-growing bulge beneath his fly. And then her resistance melted, and she was following him.

CHAPTER THIRTEEN

'I'M guessing you don't spend that much time in the quarry then?'

Stretched out horizontally across the bed, where the after-break-fast sex had left them, Millie shifted her head on Ed's stomach, luxuriating as he idly traced his finger diagonally down her back, following the tendrils of her tattoo.

Comfortable. Relaxed. Satiated. Well, almost satiated.

His deep sigh spread all the way down to her neck. 'Bit of a random comment for a Sunday morning Miss Brown. But you're right, these days I'm usually office-bound. It wasn't always like that. I started at the rock face, but as I worked my way up I spent less and less time there.' His voice trailed off with a regretful shrug, as he shuffled, adjusting his shoulders on the pillow he'd dragged over. 'It's a world-wide organisation, but mostly I'm at a screen, getting my kicks from the big deals and the big bucks, not the bangs.'

'Usually in a suit then?' She watched his amused nod, swallowed at the thought that he walked round looking that swoon-able on a daily basis. 'So how come you were in the quarry the day you rescued me?'

'Total one off, I'd bumped into Blake at my parents' party a couple of weeks earlier.' A flicker of unease ironed the folds from his cheeks. 'Blake was opening up a new section of quarry, and I came back to see the first blast for old times' sake. Blake and I go back a long way, he pulled me through my worst times.' The grin he shot her swept away the serious undertones.

'I see.' Slow conversation, to hide from scarier thoughts. Like how much sex for fun could a person have, and why did she still want more? And why, despite the no strings thing, she yearned to know more about his darker side. 'Were you bad when you were younger?'

'I was an angry teenager, I'd crashed out of school. The rest of my family were blonde and diligent, perfect achievers, and here I was, a dark, volatile hell raiser. I guess I got my temper from my Dad.' He shot her a rueful grimace. 'Blake encouraged me to turn that negative energy, into something positive. I came into the company from the rough end, but the technology was fascinating, I developed that side, and now we're world leaders in the field. Blake believed in me when no-one else could handle me. I owe him big time for that.'

'Difficult children are the strongest characters, and in the end that's a good thing, even if it's rough along the way. You got your Dad's hot temper, but I bet you got your strength from your mum.'

'Why has my mother got anything to do with this?'

One indignant reply. One mother in need of defense. 'I have a feeling she was strong, doing what she did.' She chose to ignore his scowl. 'Think about it, you'll see my point.'

One disgusted growl. 'Leave my mother out of this.' Then he went back to scratching her tattoo, making her shiver as his nail followed the sinuous stems round her side, sliding over her hip, idly stroking the skin at the edge of her stomach.

Wow, a girl could get used to this.

He cleared his throat. 'So, if it's time for twenty questions, Millie, aka Amelia Brunswick Brown, why exactly are you disowning your family?'

Wham! Out of nowhere, and her stomach contracting, and not

in a good way. Opening and closing her mouth like a guppy as she trawled her brain for an answer.

'I told you already, I want to be independent.' From his steely eyes, he knew she was flailing.

'That's a reason, not an explanation.'

Pay-back time, for pushing him.

'Maybe I couldn't take the way my parents wanted to dominate me, control my life. Take my tattoos – my mother hates them.'

All true, but a long way from *the* truth. How her parents tried to wrestle the most important decision of her life away from her. How she hated them for that, but how she hated herself more for letting it happen.

'I don't believe it's about one tattoo.'

So he wasn't buying it. Damn to that.

'This is me trying to live for myself, take responsibility for my own decisions. If I have to be financially independent to be allowed to think and do what I want, I will. I see my family from time to time, I just don't want them to support me.' She flashed a smile in his direction, hoping talking around the subject was going to shut him up. 'And living without the insulation of big money is a challenge. There are times when I miss the luxuries, but I'd rather be without them and be free. Giving stuff up isn't so difficult. It makes life more real.'

And that was only half true. Some days she enjoyed it, others it was damned hard, like when she ached for her London life, but she saw that as penance.

'I'll take your word for that. I'm not giving up my Aston or my penthouses any time soon.' He let out a hollow laugh.

'At least it gets you off the hook completely.'

'And what hook would that be?'

'You worrying I was falling for you?' She had to drive her point home here, even if it was close to the knuckle. 'I'd never choose a man with money, because I'd never want to feel I was being bought or dominated. Ed from the quarry, I might have fallen for, Ed from the board room would be out of the question.'

Peering up at Ed, and just for a moment his brow furrowed. But then it was gone.

'So, what do you say to showers then lunch?' He was sitting bolt upright, already easing himself out from under her. 'Can't say we haven't earned it.'

'Great idea.' She pushed herself up onto her elbow, expecting her smile to meet his mischievous grin half way, but he'd already turned. 'Thanks. I'll get ready.'

So that was abrupt. Here's hoping he hadn't caught the crest-fallen note in her voice. No danger of that, given the way he was crashing around.

'You can take the shower in the master suite.' He was already half way into the en-suite bathroom in this room. 'And see if you can do something about the mess whilst you're there. It's ridiculous we had to come into this suite because you'd trashed the main one. We can't swap bedrooms every time you don't feel like clearing up.'

A sudden attack from the tidy police? How they'd ended up in a different bedroom last night was a blur. She hadn't thought it had anything to do with tidy rooms.

But he wasn't there to ask.

Millie stared at the closed bathroom door, and reeled.

What the heck happened there? Pulling a sheet tight around her, she began to scour the floor for her dress and shoes.

***

Having a shower gave Millie time to reflect, and when she did think carefully about last night, she decided she could have ended up on the moon, and not been complaining. When someone did things like that to you – her body was thrumming now as she recalled O after shattering O – you really didn't give a damn where you were. And looking at the state of the master bedroom when she emerged from the bathroom, although his sudden snappiness had caught her off guard, Ed did have a point. Even by her standards, the room was chaotic.

Securing a towel around herself, she picked up a vest, folded it, and placed it on an easy chair, grabbed a stray flip flop, and rummaged under the strewn clothes to find the matching one.

'Need some help with that?'

Mr Snappy. Or should that be Mr Neat? Leaning on the door frame, all lazy and relaxed. Men with gravelly voices like that should not be allowed out. As for his low slung sweat pants, parading round in those with that body was just plain mean.

'Why? Are you offering?' Half way to slipping him a sultry smile, she caught her foot in an abandoned towel, and tripped. All down to those melting knees, and darn it that her legs weren't working at all.

His chest was hard as she barreled into it.

'Easy.' His eyes snagged onto a nipple that had escaped over the towel top, and stayed there as he righted her.

'Whoops. Sorry.' She dragged in a breath, re-adjusted her towel, and forgetting the smoulder she'd been planning, shot him one straight smile. Determined to ignore whatever was going on in the groin area of his leisure wear. 'Tidying time?

Did he have any idea how many good-boyfriend points he picked up there for offering to help? Wrong! Not boyfriend. Definitely not boyfriend. She kicked herself hard for that slip up.

'I think tidying might be a good idea. Sorry about before, if I sounded short.' He let out a sigh, as he picked up the nearest dress and began struggling to arrange the tangle of shreds. 'Part of being grown up and independent is being tidy you know. Although right now this garment, whatever it is, seems to be resisting all attempts to impose order.'

What? Had she just hear that right? First an apology, and then that. The bit about being grown up.

She screwed her head round to check if he was messing about. 'You are joking?'

'Nope, never more serious. You'd be less obsessed about the independence thing if you felt more in control, and being more organised might help.' The grin he posted her was apologetic not playful. 'I've never known anyone this untidy before.'

So what now? She would have balled him out, except maybe he did have a teensy point.

'You sound like my parents.' She stuck her hands on her hips, to make certain he got the message she wasn't happy.

'Hey, that's harsh.'

Hurt and helpful? Way too attractive. He was going to have to stop that. And she was going to have to concede he was a little bit right.

'I'll try harder in future. Hey, what are these doing here?' She scooped up one pair of exceedingly tattered jeans that had nothing to do with her, waggling them in the air triumphantly. 'These are yours mate. Kicked under the bed, no less, so it's not all my mess. I'm thinking pots, kettles, and black here.'

'Guilty as charged.' He gave a shame faced shrug.

'My favourites too.' She gave a laugh. 'Your Ed-from-the-quarry jeans. You couldn't...' No, she couldn't ask him. She wouldn't ask him. She wasn't going to beg. Even if the thought of seeing him in them with no pants was...

'What..?'

If she didn't ask now she might not ever see him in them again. One awful thought, driving her to be entirely brazen.

'Would you put them on?'

The glance he shot her was pure, delighted lust.

'Not sure I'll get the zip up.' He snatched the jeans as she flung them. 'I'll try, seeing how you asked so nicely.'

'I'd appreciate that, Mr Mitchum.' She had no idea how he'd read her ear to ear beam, as she watched him peel on the soft, oh-so-tight denims. *Rips in all the right places, and then some.*

'I take it you won't mind if lunch is an hour or two late.' He growled as he struggled to accommodate the full length of his arousal into the jeans.

'An hour or two?' She couldn't resist the tease. 'I'm not sure it's going to take that long.'

One smart smack stung her butt, and then his hot delicious mouth hit hers and she had no further sense of time at all.

***

'I think I'm getting the idea of this no-strings fun thing.'

Millie sauntered across the village square beside him, flip flops flipping, bumping him gently as her hips swayed, stripping the last of an ice lolly off a stick with a tongue-technique so enticing, he decided he'd rather look away.

'Yep, I thought you might. Just a shame we lost most of yesterday. A weekend should be plenty to burn out the heat, but we'll be struggling if you're off home tomorrow. Always best to do it in one hit, and move on.' He pushed the end of his own Cornetto into his mouth, and crunched it.

And always, best to tell it like it is.

Which was why he was ignoring Millie's appalled expression and bashing on with the home truths. Except it wasn't exactly the truth. Because he seldom made a whole weekend of it, and he'd never spent the length of time he'd spent with Millie, with anyone. And he'd never had this much sex with one person. Another reason why it was so strange that this far through the weekend, instead of feeling the burn was subsiding, he had the uncomfortable impression it was getting hotter.

'Shall we walk up through the village to the church at the top?' Although she'd moved a pace away from him, her dismayed expression had morphed to bright and airy.

'Good idea, the vista's meant to be amazing, and seeing as this village is off the main tourist trail, at least its quiet. Will you be okay on the cobbles in those sandals?'

Cobbles spinning him back to the polished, well groomed awesome Millie, who'd powered her way through his mother's reception yesterday evening, and gone on to power him right over the edge. He felt himself stiffening now at the thought of her slinking around the kitchen. But that untouchable, sultry Millie had dematerialised as soon as her high heels and dress had hit the deck, and she'd been eager and insatiable as he was. Not forgetting those amazing stockings. Strange though, the Millie he preferred was the Millie he had here, all raw, and vulnerable. Crumpled, yet real.

'Heels and cobbles don't mix, but flip flops are good.' The smile she flipped him, made his heart...

Squeezing. Flopping. Thumping. Whatever. Hearts were off limits. Totally.

Unless like last night, they were racing because of the lust, and the sex.

Then it was okay.

Hard to think this time yesterday he'd been enduring the whole damned challenge without any of the benefits. Millie's u-turn on the sex-front had come as one big bonus. And the other plus was that the end of the challenge was in sight. Only the family meet left, and no idea at all how he was going to engineer that as yet. Then he'd be paying Will and Cassie a visit, to rub their noses in his victory.

Winding their way up in the shade of the narrow alleys, picking their way past geranium pots, his hand fell easily onto the small of her back. 'It's quite a climb, are you okay?'

'I dance, remember? I have stamina. I bet I could beat you to the top.' A toss of her head, one challenging grin, and she was off.

There was no way that he could catch her now.

She reached the top first, barely panting. Blowing her damp fringe upwards, she flopped down onto a bench in dappled shade, and he dropped beside her.

'Worth getting out of breath for that view.' He was talking about the patterns of pan-tiled roofs and the rolling plains beyond, but focusing on her tanned thighs, spreading on the warm stone seat.

'You know what else is a waste?'

'No, but I'm sure you're going to tell me anyway.' Sometimes she reminded him a lot of Cassie, and not in a good way. The way she never let things rest.

'You being on your own is a waste.' She stretched her legs out in front of her, oblivious to his eyebrows hitting the sky as her words hit home. 'You're a lovely guy. When you forget about being grumpy you're fun, you're kind, and you're great in bed. Not for me, obviously. But somehow I think you'd enjoy life more with a partner than on your own.'

Right about her sounding like Cassie then.

'Don't you start too.' He regretted that the moment it slipped out.

She pounced. 'Why, who else says it?'

'Pretty much everyone.' Hopefully that fudged it, but it was dangerously close to challenge territory. 'They're all wanting to get me married off.'

'And you're resisting because of the commitment thing?'

'What commitment thing would that be?'

'You not wanting to commit because of your abandonment issues.'

'My what?' Where the heck had that come from, and more to the point, where the heck was it going?

'It's obvious. You avoid relationships because you think your mother left you. You're probably scared of being left again.'

'Thank you Mrs Freud, but that has nothing to do with it.'

'Don't you think you should get your Mother's side of the story? It's not like you don't know who she is?'

'Definitely not.'

'Well has anyone else in the family talked to her about it?'

'Lizzie – that's my birth mother – doesn't see anyone in the family. Never has, although Cassie looked her up a few years ago, when she was in the States.'

'There you go then. And?'

'I didn't ask, I'm not interested.'

'Really Ed. You are the limit. How are you going to get on with your life if you don't sort this out?'

'I wasn't aware there was anything *to* sort until two minutes ago.' He heard his voice crack with indignation. 'What's it got to do with you anyway?'

She screwed up her face, let out a deep sigh.

'You're right, it's nothing to do with me.' She put a hand on his arm, and he winced at the screaming-pink nails. 'I'm sorry, I shouldn't have said anything, wouldn't have. It's just I'm going back tomorrow, so it seemed like a now-or-never moment.'

'Never might have been good.' He shrugged, rubbing his chin. 'You don't have to leave tomorrow.'

A couple of extra days to extinguish their fire. And it wasn't only about the burn-out. If they travelled back through London, they could pull in a visit to her family, and tick the last box of the challenge. And then it would be over. If he pulled this off, he'd be a free man by Wednesday. Whoop, whoop. Way to go Ed! So now he needed a charm offensive to persuade her. Except it was never quite that simple. Second guessing Millie's reactions was a science that was beyond him.

'We could always stay. One more day to go for burn-out. What do you say?' He tried to read her reaction, but she avoided his gaze, sat her biting her lip, tapping her feet in silence.

Millie lost for words? That was a new one.

Impatient for a result, he pushed her. 'So?'

Her hand was on his arm again, bright nails fluttering. 'Thanks for the offer. Another couple of days would be great but...' Her wistful tone became apologetic, but firm. 'Probably best to leave things as they are.'

Dammit. Why was there always a 'but'?

'Let's wander down before we decide.' He stood up, offered a hand to pull her to her feet. 'You might have changed your mind by the time we reach the bottom.'

And, just as likely, not. She was going to make him work for this, like she had all along. But, he was man enough for the challenge, and if he had to dig deep, then he would.

CHAPTER FOURTEEN

MILLIE had no idea how that happened. One minute they were in a sleepy hill village, and a scant hour later they were on a hotel terrace under stripy parasols, watching the sun spark off the ocean.

'Thought you'd enjoy a glimpse of the Med...' Ed narrowed his eyes at her, his glass of mineral water half way to his lips. 'Before you head home, if that's what you're still insisting you're going to do.'

Damn. She'd meant to dive in and talk about the bright blue sea. 'I thought we'd agreed we weren't going to mention that again.'

'You might have. I didn't.'

'You never give up do you?'

A waiter approached with a glorious seafood platter. Hopefully that would shut Ed up for a bit. Not that she wasn't tempted. She'd left next week free, hoping to get on with her boxes, her regular classes were on summer break. She didn't have to rush back, and since they'd sorted out what was – or wasn't – going on, she was having a great time. But perhaps she was enjoying it all too much. If she left tomorrow, she could count the weekend as her first no-strings achievement. But any longer than that, and she was scared she'd get too used to his easy ways, not to mention those dynamite orgasms. Some things a girl could have too much of, and it was nothing at all to do with caring, or falling for someone. Ed might have his own worries on that score, imagining that she was going to get all clingy and difficult, but he couldn't have been less wrong, because she had no space for a man in her life, and that was definite. But when the good things weren't there any more you'd miss them too much. And no way was she going to risk that.

So Mr Mitchum had to accept she was leaving tomorrow, end of.

Across the table, Ed inclined his head. 'I know they aren't your favourite people, but do you see much of your family?'

That arrived out of nowhere. Except Ed rarely made small-talk for no reason. She put down the king prawn in front of her, and met his gaze.

'Where is this going exactly?' She licked a salty finger.

He shook his head blithely. 'Nowhere.'

'Sorry, I don't buy that.' She scowled him a dead eye.

'So when *did* you last see them?' The line of his jaw said he wasn't backing down.

Damn this man.

'A while ago. I'm busy, I don't go south much.' Suitably imprecise, and excuses to match. 'Why has it got anything to do with you anyway?'

The memory of holding Sophie's new-born baby still turned her heart to dry ice. *That echo, in the space where her own baby should have been.*

'No reason.' He gave a nonchalant shrug. 'Are they in London then?'

Would he never give up?

'Okay, last reply on the subject. My little sister is at uni, my parents are in Knightsbridge, my older sister Sophie lives in Belsize Park.' Sucking the sour saliva out of her mouth, she forced herself to say it. 'She's the one with the baby.'

If he'd noticed her voice had dropped to a whisper, he didn't react.

'I'm picking up a family estrangement vibe here.' Ignoring her

163

appalled frown, he bashed on regardless. 'Why don't we fly back to London on Wednesday, and drop in on Sophie? Then I'll run you back up north afterwards. It's good to touch base with your siblings, even if you have issues with your parents.' He flashed her a triumphant beam.

Talk about insensitive.

'Sorry, an hour ago we were talking about you needing to see Cassie to find out what happened when your real mother left you. How did we come from that to this?'

Seeing his jaw sag, she hoped she hadn't been too harsh. But he was asking for it.

'Right. You have me there.' He pursed his lips, pushed his fingertips together. 'Cassie lives in Camden. Not far away. We could see them both?'

Now he was talking randomly. What the heck was this about?

'Okay, you may like this better.' He fished his phone out of his pocket, and flicked some buttons. 'There's a flea-market in Nimes on Monday, and Aix on Tuesday. We could go to those too?'

This man knew her too well. Two more flea markets? That *was* temptation.

'No point. I'm maxed out on all my cards.'

'Don't take this the wrong way, but I could fund a bit of shopping...' Noting her expression, he rephrased. 'As a loan if you'd prefer.'

Why was he pulling out all the stops here? Oh my. Surely not? Kerching! The sound of the penny dropping. He was so determined to burn this thing out, he was throwing every enticement he could her way. A man who didn't take no for an answer, with no clue how much she didn't want to see her sister.

She drew in a deep breath, bracing herself to test him. There was one deal she would be interested in brokering, if only to see this whole thing through. In a weird way she felt like she owed it to him. Whatever else he'd done, he'd helped her put Josh firmly behind her, and she'd always be grateful to him for that. And that was before you even got on to the bit about showing her she was capable of a climax. Whatever his shortcomings, she'd be returning home a different woman. And if she could pull this off, she'd set him on the way to a better future too.

'I'm not agreeing to anything here, but try this for size. How about I stay until Wednesday, then on the way back we can go and find out what Cassie knows about your birth mother.'

The oyster he'd just picked up clattered back onto his plate.

He screwed up his face. Three, four, five long seconds. Not happy about this then. Eight, nine, ten, then he shifted, clenched his jaw, stared her straight in the eye.

'And we'll see Sophie at the same time?'

Oh, the way those dark eyes made her stomach descend. Not good news.

'That wasn't part of it. Why are you so keen for me to see Sophie?'

He gave yet another diffident shrug. 'Maybe the same reason you want me to see Cassie – because I have a gut instinct that in the long run it'll be in your best interest. I know you might have been jealous of her as a child, but it would be useful to put that behind you, and I think you know that too. Nothing like sorting out family stuff.' He gave a wry grimace, then stretched across the white damask tablecloth, caught her wrist between his fingers. 'So, do we have a deal?'

Oh my. Bulls and china shops springing to mind. Crashing about, and him with no idea about any of it. He couldn't find out the truth, about what had happened. Nobody could. She let out a smooth breath.

Give and take. Isn't that what it was all about? Something for him, something for her, although heaven knows how she was going to carry off seeing Sophie and the baby. And definitely not thinking about the heat-burning that was going to go down the next few days. Ignoring the smile lines crinkling in the corners of his eyes, ignoring the twist of those destructively sensuous lips, she locked onto his deep, dark pupils.

'I'd say we have a deal, Mr Mitchum.'

***

Millie had travelled in style with her parents, but it was never quite so smooth as flying into London later that week with Ed. She'd insisted on keeping her personal travel bag with her. The rest of her parcels had been whisked away, with the promise that they'd be back home before she was. And once the private jet landed, she still felt like her feet hadn't touched the ground.

'You okay over there?' Ed glanced up from his laptop, lobbed another of those melting smiles she still wasn't immune to, across the back seat of the limo. 'You don't mind if I check my mail? There's a big deal going through today.'

'I'm fine. Enjoying the scenery. Crossing London always feels like coming home.' She shot him wry grin, curled her feet more tightly underneath her. 'Even the North Circular has a certain glamour when you've been deprived of it. And it's good that the sun's out, even if the sky isn't as blue as in Provence.'

Good thing it was all happening at the speed of light, not giving her any time to think about the heavy ache in her chest. And the stony drag in her gut had to be down to the flight, and not anything to do with the fact she was dreading saying goodbye to Ed, being back on her own again. Dammit. She gave herself a mental kick. This was exactly what she should have avoided. *She was not attached to Ed. Definitely not.* Once she was home again, and busy, she'd be fine.

At least this far she had managed not to worry too much about seeing Sophie. And Bella, the baby. The thought of Bella was much worse. But now, as they turned into Camden Square, yesterday's butterflies morphed into a flock of seagulls, and as they drifted to a halt outside the house, the bird-wings began flapping, wildly.

Swallowing hard, she groped for the boots she'd kicked off earlier.

Now was not the time to deposit that delicious in-flight lunch on the limo seat.

'Nice place they've got here.' Ed next to her on the back seat nodded his appreciation.

'Yes, Rob's family own a bank or something, and it's a lovely house, they've been here three years.' No idea how she was getting the words out at all, let alone how she was sounding so nonchalant.

'C'mon you, we're already running late.' Not waiting for the chauffeur, Ed was out the second the car stopped, and hauling her onto the pavement the next, then Sophie was there too, baby Bella on her hip, ushering them through the wide front door into the house in a flurry of hugs and kisses.

If Sophie was surprised by their visit she didn't let on, as she led the way into the elegant lounge, now humanised by toys scattered across the designer rugs and sofas. She was as friendly as she had been when Millie had rung to say they were coming. A little more rounded, a little less perfectly groomed than before, yet glowing and relaxed – being a mum suited her. Millie sighed inwardly as she settled on the edge of a velvet sofa, tried to stop her chest imploding. Whatever her own pain, she didn't begrudge Sophie her happiness.

'There aren't many days when we're home alone, are there Bella?' Sophie dropped a kiss on Bella's head, lowered her to the floor, and the child shot off on all fours, making a bee-line for Ed.

167

Across the room, Millie sat, in silence. Gritting her teeth. Keeping hold, arms wrapped tight around her stomach. She'd promised herself she wouldn't do it. She mustn't compare Bella to the baby she herself might have had. Bella wasn't even a baby now, she was a living, breathing person, demanding, exacting. She was just eight months younger than hers would have been, and everyone was so right that she couldn't have coped alone. *Could she?* She bit back the lump in her throat, took a jagged breath, and knew she'd been right to stay away. She'd only seen Bella once, briefly, just after she'd been born. But she had to be strong now. So long as she kept her distance here she'd cope.

From the way she was eyeballing Ed, Bella already had a huge will of her own.

What was it about that man and his magnetism?

'Watch out, she could be sticky!' Sophie's warning came too late. Bella was already hauling herself up, wiping her hands all over Ed's trouser leg.

'Don't worry.' He picked up a teddy from the floor and waggled it in Bella's direction, receiving squawks of laughter in return.

'Hazard of babies, I forget not everyone's used to it.' Sophie glowed appreciatively in Ed's direction. 'Wow, she's taken to you.'

'I've got an army of nephews and nieces.' He gave a laid back chuckle, as Bella grasped his finger, and set about gnawing on the sleeve of his jacket. 'That's why I'm used to baby slobber.'

As she watched this chilled, child-friendly Ed, Millie struggled to keep her eyes from popping out of her head. Who'd have thought? A hoard of nephews and nieces she hadn't even heard about. Although there was no reason why she should have. She'd had four short days of wickedness with him – that was all she'd had, all she was going to have. If there was a tiny twang of regret that it wouldn't be more, she wasn't about to acknowledge it. That army of nieces and nephews would be for someone else to discover, not her.

'Shall I go and make some drinks, seeing as I'm the free one here?' Millie stood up, smoothed her hands over the crumples in her dress, and moved towards the door. An excuse for escape, as she desperately tried to banish the image of Josh's thunderous face, the morning she emerged from the bathroom with a pregnancy testing stick in her hand. Those two blue lines, shaping her future. That had been the day he walked out on her.

'That would be wonderful.' The lightness of Sophie's words were at odds with her concerned frown. 'Shout if there's anything you can't find.'

By the time Millie returned with a tray of drinks, Bella was snuggled on Ed's lap, exploring his pockets.

'I thought we'd stick to cold drinks.' Millie handed Sophie a glass, clunked Ed's on the table beside him, and headed back to her chair.

She sneaked a look at her watch as she sipped her juice. They were due at Cassie's by three. Ten more minutes and they'd be heading off. Not so much more to endure.

'Hey, watch out Ed, there's nothing Bella loves more than keys.' Sophie laughed, as Bella grabbed Ed's keys, and he tried unsuccessfully to wrestle them back. 'I can see she's already got you wrapped around her little finger.'

Millie watched guardedly, letting out a sigh of relief as Ed moved to get up. Great, they were leaving even earlier than she thought.

Sophie held out her arms to take Bella from Ed. But instead he set off towards Millie, and in two strides he was in front of her.

Behind him, Millie saw Sophie's face crumple in desperation, but she was helpless.

'Come and talk to Auntie Millie whilst I have my juice.'

Millie gasped as a warm, squirming Bella hit her full in the solar plexus, and the smell of clean baby enveloped her in a sickening cloud. 'Oh my!'

Don't panic! Don't hyperventilate!

One squishy hand hit her chin, then Bella's head hit her chest, and easy as that, she was cuddling her. Not so hard.

Sophie lurched across the room. 'I'm so sorry Mills.'

And somewhere beyond that, Ed was back in his chair, a beatific smile on his face.

'All okay Mills?' Sophie swooped on Bella, disentangling sticky clutching fingers from Millie's hair. 'Hey, someone needs changing!'

And then it was over, and Millie began to breathe again.

'We'd better be heading off, if that's okay with you Millie?' Ed was already standing, tucking in his shirt, clicking his keys.

And in a blur, they were in the hall, spilling out of the door, Ed tickling Bella's fingers as he said goodbye.

'Okay?' Sophie spoke under her breath as she cradled Millie's shoulder with her spare arm, and patted her, anxiously. Then she raised her voice again, and a quizzical eyebrow. 'One great guy you've found here Mills.'

'He's not mine, really he's not.' *And really not wishing he was.*

'I believe you, thousands wouldn't.' Sophie waved from the doorstep. 'Take care, see you guys again soon.'

Out on the pavement, beyond the neat designer hedge, Millie blinked in the afternoon sun, and let out a long shuddering sigh, which came to a premature end as she realised the limo was drawing away.

'Where's the car going Ed?'

Smothering a grin, he pushed his hand into his pocket, tossed his keys into the air.

'Change of vehicle, I'm afraid.' He nodded towards a sleek sports car. 'I had it brought here whilst we were inside. I need to show this baby to my best friend Will. He'll be at Cassie's later – just to dangle it in front of him, make him jealous, you understand.'

Now she'd heard it all. She scoured his face in disbelief. 'Guys do stuff like that?'

'Yes, they do.' He flashed her an unapologetic smirk. 'And before you get in, I need a solid assurance you aren't going to put your feet on the upholstery.'

She snorted. 'I can walk.'

'Now you're being silly.' He held the door open for her. 'Jump in, and hold on tight.'

So cosy baby-cuddler had legged it, and testosterone-fuelled macho-man was here in his place.

She sniffed, to emphasise how un-impressed she was.

'Sounds more like a plane than a car.' Her head jerked against the head rest as Ed pulled away, and a nano second later they screeched to a halt at the end of the road.

He grinned across at her, as they pulled out into the line of traffic. 'That went well then.'

'As you said after your mother's soiree, it depends who you are, and where you were standing.' She returned his grin, less shaky now. 'I'm just glad it's over.'

'Well, you and Sophie were great, there were no tensions, I didn't pick up any jealousy vibes at all.'

'Jealousy? Who said anything about jealousy?' She stared at him, incredulous, hearing her voice soaring high. 'You thought that's why I didn't want to see Sophie?'

Damn, damn, damn. Why had she said that? It was out before she could stop it.

'Well if it wasn't jealousy, why the hell was it?' The sideways glance he shot her bore straight to her soul.

Millie avoided his eye, stared out of the window.

That was one secret she couldn't share with anyone.

CHAPTER FIFTEEN

ED could tell from the way Cassie was swishing that she was in her element. She'd swished them into the house when they arrived, swished them out into the garden with the cream tea and straw-berries, and even though they'd collapsed onto the easy chairs in the shade of the apple tree now, she was still damn well swishing.

'Isn't this lovely?' She beamed down at them, in a way that made his blood boil, and even though he was the victor here, and this was the final set-piece of the challenge, he wasn't enjoying rubbing her nose in it half as much as he'd anticipated. He shot a sideways glance at Millie, sitting in the next chair, coolly winding her dress strands around her fingers, and grimaced. At least she was holding up well in the face of the whirlwind that was Cassie Mitchum.

'It might be lovely if you'd sit down.'

He guessed the real satisfaction was going to come when he showed Will the car that he wasn't going to surrender, because, as predicted, he'd completed every step of the challenge, and managed not to fall in love. Not even come close.

'Okay, keep your hair on.' Cassie posted him one filthy look, as with one last twirl, she collapsed into a chair beside them.

Millie was laughing openly now.

Ed rounded on her. 'What's wrong with you, Millie?'

She pursed away the laughter. 'Are you two always like this?

You've been like squabbling ten tear olds ever since we arrived.'

'Good point, well made Millie.' Cassie glared at him. 'Ed is always impossible.'

So ridiculous, he decided to let that go.

Millie cleared her throat. 'So did Ed tell you why we've come Cassie?'

'Sorry?' Cassie on the spot, opening and closing her pretty mouth.

Ed cut in, before Millie could elaborate. 'I didn't because I thought we might not actually...'

Millie's eye-roll said she wasn't going to let him off that lightly.

'If Ed's determined not to ask, I will.' Millie raised her eyebrows at Cassie, and drew in a long breath. 'You saw Lizzie, when you were in America – did she mention anything about Ed?'

Go straight for the jugular, why don't you.

Millie spun to Cassie. 'You will tell us if you know anything won't you Cassie, because it's important for Ed to know.'

'Oh dear.' Cassie sniffed deeply, chewed on her thumb as she hesitated. 'I did see Lizzie, four years ago. I was traveling in the States, and I wasn't even sure she'd agree to see me, but she did and we spent a couple of nights together. It wasn't until the last night that she mentioned anything about you Ed. At first I thought she wasn't going to, but in the end I had the feeling she was relieved to talk about it – finally. I was the first person in the family she'd ever agreed to see, apparently.'

Millie rounded on her fiercely. 'So why didn't you tell Ed when you came back?'

With fire-power like that, Ed was pleased Millie was fighting for him not against him.

'Lizzie asked me not to say anything. And you know how Ed is.' Cassie sent her a conspiratorial grimace. 'Impossible at the best of times. Even if Lizzie had asked me to tell him everything, he wouldn't have listened. So it was easier to leave it. That way I wasn't breaking Lizzie's confidence, and I wasn't really short-changing Ed either. What she said was fairly shocking, and I didn't want to hurt people.' She gave a shivery shrug, offered a weak smile of excuse.

Ed blocked the constricting waves gripping his stomach. 'So let's get it over with. What the hell did she say?'

Cassie stared at her fingers. 'When she got pregnant she was sixteen, with a really promising academic future. Mum and Dad were appalled, and she fought them to let her have the baby. They eventually agreed, but only on condition she gave the baby up and let them adopt it. Then they insisted she got on with her life.'

'Hang on, this isn't an 'it' we're talking about, this is me!'

Cassie carried on as if she hadn't heard him.

'Lizzie was so furious with them, the only way she could handle it was by leaving completely. She kept contact to the bare minimum, because she said when she was in America, the pain was further away. Now she's older, she doesn't blame our parents, she knows they had her best interests at heart. She did marry, but she didn't have any more children, because she knew that if anything happened to them she couldn't go through the pain of losing another child. I think she always hoped you would contact her. For what it's worth, I got the feeling being made to give you up pretty much broke her.'

'Okay.' Ed rubbed a thumb hard across his forehead struggling to take it in.

Except when had any of it ever been okay? At least he knew now.

So Millie had been right all along. Grinding his teeth, as the garden and the warm afternoon flickered in and out of focus. *His mother hadn't left him. Not voluntarily.* His guts had momentarily dematerialised, and when he opened his mouth to speak, there weren't any words. When he finally looked up Millie was staring at him, her cheeks blotchy and wet.

'I told you Ed, I knew she was strong.' She sniffed and rubbed the back of her hand across her eyes. 'She had you because she loved you, and she didn't choose or mean to leave you. She did it because she was made to.'

So that had wiped the smile off Cassie's face. Just for once, bubbly, irrepressible, hideously annoying Cassie wasn't bouncing. And for once she wasn't gloating either. All of them, sitting under the apple tree, staring at the patches of blue sky through the gaps in the leaves. Not saying anything, because what the hell was there to say.

Ed slapped a hand to his head, as his body finally began to respond to his brain again. 'So all my life I've hated her for something that wasn't her fault. What a screw-up.' He brought his fist down, and banged his knee.

Feeling the pressure of a light hand on his forearm now. *Millie.* Letting him know it was all good, that he could move through the anger that had been devouring his soul his whole life. That at last he would be able to trust, because just as Millie had said, none of it had been his mother's choice.

Sliding around to watch Millie now. Make-up smudges under her eyes, hair like a tornado just passed through, anxiously rubbing her thumb over that pout. This unassuming, scruff of a girl who, one last time, had flipped his life upside down. *How the hell did she keep doing that?* As she caught his eye, her lips curved into the smallest, sweetest smile of encouragement that turned his legs molten in a heartbeat. He pushed that thought right to the back of his head and buried it. Fast. Under a mental rock fall. Even now she was effortlessly, sexy as hell, firing a rocket of latent lust through his groin, yet full of more goodness than anyone he'd ever known. Remembering what they were actually doing here, a yank of guilt ripped through his gut.

Here they were, waiting for Will, to wrap up the challenge,

Millie, sitting there all raw, and soft, yet so wise and honest and strong, and somehow this was entirely the wrong place for her to be. A rush of shame engulfed him as he thought of the challenge. How cheap did that make him, faced with a woman of Millie's integrity? The whole damn thing that had begun so harmlessly now showed him his true colours, sordid, tawdry and disgusting beside the amazing woman he'd been using. This was no place for Millie. A woman like her deserved so much better than this.

'C'mon Millie.' He grasped the chair arms decisively. 'Let's get you out of here, I'm taking you home.'

Somewhere on the periphery of his vision, Cassie began to flap her hands in protest. 'But aren't you waiting for Will, I'm sure he won't be long? What about the...'

Excellent question Cassie – and what about the challenge? How about stuff the damned challenge, right where it belonged, so it didn't bring down a decent woman like Millie. Why the hell had he gone through with it? How the hell had he been so blind? When had harmless fun turned so damned cheap?

'Millie's back at work tomorrow, and there are things I need to tell her.' Ignoring Millie's wide-eyed query, he grasped her wrist. One tug, and she flew her out of her chair, her thigh crashing into his as she stumbled beside him. He was ready to make any bad excuse he could to get her out of here, and fast. 'Best get off, then we'll miss the worst of the traffic.'

'Now you are being ridiculous Ed, its rush hour...'

Cassie could protests as much as she wanted, he was out of here.

'We'll take our chances, thanks for the tea.' He was already diving through the house, dragging Millie behind him. As soon as they were in the calm of the car he would come clean about the challenge.

Pushing Millie in front of him now, down the steps towards the car, as Cassie arrived, panting, clutching at his elbow.

'Bye Millie, lovely to meet you, see you again soon!' Cassie's face folded into an anxious frown, as she murmured at his shoulder. 'Aww, she's so right for you. Whatever you do Ed, don't mention you know... The thing Will was coming for. Not to Millie.'

So typical of Cassie, never knowing when to stop meddling in his life.

'Cut out the match-making Cassie. The challenge is over, and coming clean with Millie is the least I can do.' He swept her hand away, and jumped the steps in one. 'At least that way it ends honestly.'

'Telling a woman that you only went out with her for a bet – you might as well give her a slap in the face.' Her bright blue eyes were piercing and angry. 'If you tell Millie that, you really don't deserve her.'

As he swept towards the car, he could still see Cassie in doorway, red-faced and perplexed, and he fought the inner child in him, who still wanted to prove her wrong, at every turn.

He snorted dismissively. What did Cassie know anyway?

***

Ed usually found the cream interior of the Aston simultaneously calming and empowering, with its sleek leather seats and the robust instrument panel, but as they roared away from Cassie's house he was anything but calm or empowered. In control at all times was how he liked to be, and right now he had the sense that his control was spiraling away from him. He snatched a glance at Millie, just to check she had both feet firmly on the floor. The way his life was unravelling right now, one careless girlie foot on a seat could easily push him over the edge.

'Are you okay with what Cassie said about your mum?' Her

hand slipped onto his knee, gentle, caring, echoing the concern in her voice.

'I will be.' Eventually. When he'd stopped reeling, when he'd had time to assimilate, he was sure he'd feel better about it. 'Thanks for making me come today, for making me ask.' He shot her a glance he hoped was grateful enough.

'I hope you didn't rush away for me.' Millie spoke, then wound around to watch him. 'It's amazing that you're taking me home at all, when it's a three hundred mile round trip. There's no hurry.'

He shrugged, and grimaced as the traffic slid from a crawl to a halt, hammering his fingers on the steering wheel. 'Good thing, given the gridlock.'

Damn that they were stuck, when all he wanted was to let rip, roar up the motorway.

'But I thought you wanted to stay to see Will – didn't you bring the car specially?'

And there he had it, the perfect opening. He inhaled, to psych himself up, knowing he'd feel better when he'd done it. He owed it to Millie to be honest, and if any woman would understand, she would.

'There's something I need to tell you about that.' He threw a nervous glance, and fleetingly, met her eye. For a second the way she was sitting there, all soft and trusting, flipped his stomach. This was no time for him to go chicken. So long as he missed out the jibe about his bed conveyor-belt bed, if he put the right spin on it, he was sure he could make the whole thing sound above board.

'Will and I had this bet. We were at a party, and he was going on about how I'd never had a steady girlfriend, and how he was sure I couldn't manage ten dates with one woman. And I was sure I could.'

He flung a desperate grimace towards her.

'So what's this to do with me?'

He bashed on, cutting her off.

'It sounds worse than it is. It was a challenge, there were incentives – houses, cars.' He wished it didn't sound so crass. 'It was a ridiculous guy thing, that got out of hand, and I should never have involved you.'

This was not coming out well.

'Are you saying I'm part of some bet of yours?'

Her brow was furrowed with disbelief, but at least she wasn't shouting, although something in the detached chill of her voice sent warning shivers spiraling down his spine. Dammit, yelling would be a better option.

'I'm so sorry, Millie, it was meant to be fun, you weren't ever meant to know. But after what we shared this afternoon, I wanted to tell you.' He watched, in horror, as she reached down and unclipped her seat belt, flailing for something to say in his defense. 'Cassie said I shouldn't say anything, but it didn't seem fair not to. I'm trying to do the decent thing, to be honest.'

He was going from bad to worse here, given the way her face was folding in disgust.

'Cassie was in this too?' Her voice soared indignantly. She scrabbled, turning to kneel on the seat, as she reached into the back of the car, grabbing at her case. 'Now I've heard it all.'

'It isn't as bad as it looks.' He ducked as her travel bag swung past his ear. 'What the hell are you doing, Millie?'

'What does it look like I'm doing?' She spat the words through gritted teeth, as she flung the door open. 'I'm getting out of the car, and then I'm going home. On my own.' She was already on the pavement, slamming the door, hair mussed all over her face, running, already merging with the crowds as they swarmed towards the nearby Underground entrance.

'Wait Millie, I can explain...' Ed was out of the car and lunging across the road, but in the two seconds it took to reach the pavement, Millie had gone.

Damn, damn, damn. Why the heck did he do this right outside a tube station? If he'd had half a brain he'd have waited until they were on the motorway. He closed his eyes, shook his head. He could try to follow her, but given the crowds he had little chance of finding her. And if he did catch her up, would she even speak to him?

Would she hell.

Horns were blaring from the road now, irate drivers blasting at his driverless car. Giving up was not his style, but chasing Millie here was pointless.

Cursing, he threw himself back towards his car.

***

'Hi there stranger, what happened to Derbyshire then?'

Will looked up nonchalantly from his seat under Cassie's apple tree, his greeting grin fading as he took in Ed's scowl.

'Derbyshire just got blown skywards, all my fault.' Ed threw himself into the chair, and kicked out his feet. 'Where's Cassie anyway?' At least she wasn't here to gloat.

'She disappeared when she heard you come back. You can hear the Aston engine approaching from miles away. Muttered something about keeping out of boys business.' Will rolled his eyes. 'I guess she's talking about this challenge you just nailed. How did it go then?'

Ed shrugged. 'How about the hardest thing I've done, in my whole life – I reckon that covers it.'

'That's it? Cassie said Millie went down a storm with everyone.'

'Pretty much.' Except for him, that was. 'She turned my life upside down and shook it – hard. I guess anyone who saw it

180

found that amusing.'

He twisted his mouth into a rueful, self-deprecating smile. No way was he going to tell Will he felt like he'd cut off his arm now that Millie wasn't here, even though it was barely fifteen minutes since she left.

'Cassie says you brought the Aston along, just to show me what I wasn't going to get.'

'Exactly. Eat your heart out Will, I failed to fall in love, so the Aston's still mine.'

'Nice twist that, not that I ever expected to get my hands on it. I mean, who'd fall in love, after ten dates with a random woman?'

Something in Will's throwaway tone made his chest tighten.

'Millie's not a random woman. She's individual, strong, compassionate, compelling, interesting, sparky. She might be a right royal pain in the butt, but she's got more integrity in her little finger than the rest of us put together.'

'Whoa, no need to take it personally.' Will swallowed and raised his eyebrows, shuffling uneasily. 'Whatever she is, whoever she is, she's won you my flat in Klosters fair and square, and who'd have thought that would be possible? Ed Mitchum, having ten dates with the same woman. That must qualify as some kind of miracle in itself. I'll have the flat transferred to you as soon as...'

Ed shook his head. 'You can keep your flat. I've got to the end of it, but I'm certainly not accepting the spoils.'

A whole afternoon of images were flashing through Ed's head now, all of them featuring Millie. The easy way she'd thrown her head back, laughing when she met Cassie, almost as if she was coming home. That secret smile of reassurance, sent just for him when he was crashing, as he took in the news about his mother. The way her eyes went blurry every time he made her come. Not strictly from this afternoon, but he kept seeing it anyway. But there was one image his brain had on lock-on repeat – Millie, her arms

181

wrapped protectively around the baby on her knee, and that one made his throat constrict, and his guts do a double somersault.

Then there was that final, killing, expression of hurt confusion which spread across her face when he dropped the bombshell about the challenge. And every time the loop stopped on that one, his mouth filled with sour saliva, and he thought he was going to throw up.

'Okay, take a chill pill. It's over now, it's not important, let's forget it, and move on.' Will got to his feet. 'Fancy a beer?'

'Nope, I'll head off. I'm off to South America tomorrow, to sort out some deals.'

All planned, and put in place, to make sure he didn't waver after the whole extended weekend of fun. To make sure the fun didn't drag on any more, because, when it came to it, he almost hadn't wanted it to end at all.

'I didn't know you were going away so soon.'

'I need to get back to work. I've had two weeks away from the business, and when did I last do that?'

'When did you ever do that?' Will stared at him hard, through narrowing eyes.

Ed had been thinking of the South American trip as cooling off time, a chance to reassess – how he felt, what he wanted, where he was going. Except now none of that mattered now, because he'd totally blown it with Millie. No one who looked at you with that much disdain as they ran away from you was going to reconsider anything. The vision of the hurt in her eyes flashed through his head again, this time with the addition of a knife that twisted, and sent a stabbing pain deep into his chest.

'South America – there's a whole un-tapped market for our latest blasting software I need to check it out.' Throwing a line to Will here, buying himself a minute to think.

'I'm sure.'

Will, laconic as usual, tapping his fingers on the chair arm.

A trip to South America? Cooling off time? A chance to reassess? Ed gave himself a mental kick. How stupid was he? Twenty minutes without Millie, and he already knew.

He was in love with her, damn it.

When the hell had that happened? And how? No idea, apart from the fact that it finally clicked when he saw her with the baby. That pretty much blew his mind. The whole rush through his body, at the realisation he wanted her to have his children. All afternoon, he'd tried to blank it out, suppress the thought... But it was true. At least it gave a rational explanation for why the heat between them was burning like an inferno, when it should have been dying embers. How the hell could he be expected to recognise love, when he'd never known it before?

And typical Millie, as if it isn't enough that she doesn't want a man in her life at all, contrary as usual, she had to choose this moment to decide that he was the one man in the world she despised.

Standing up, Ed fished in his pocket for the keys to the Aston, and tossed them casually towards Will.

'I think these are yours.'

Will snatched them out of the air, his brows knitting quizzically. 'Meaning?'

Ed snorted. How slow could a guy be?

'Meaning I'm giving you the damned Aston after all. It's yours, because it's the end of the goddam challenge, and scrub what I said before – I've fallen in love. I'm in love with Millie Brown, and before you ask, no, she doesn't know, and I don't have the first idea what I'm going to do about it either.'

CHAPTER SIXTEEN

'IF you didn't insist on rolling in the dirt Cracker, you'd get out for your ride a while lot sooner.'

Millie bent her head against the pony's flank, rubbing at the dried mud vigorously with a brush. There was something very soothing about talking to a pony, and ever since she got back from the dreaded trip to Provence, she'd been pouring her woes out to Cracker.

'Good thing you're a good listener, isn't it boy?' She slapped his rump, and he gave her bare knee a nuzzle as she headed off to get his tack.

The thing was, all the pony nuzzles in the world weren't going to make her feel better. Since she'd got back she couldn't sleep, couldn't concentrate, and was bursting into tears whenever her favourite songs came on the radio. And it wasn't just seeing Bella again. She'd written the whole trip off as one big disaster, hurled it into her never-think-of-it-again box, and slammed the lid firmly. But it was refusing to stay there.

So much for a fun weekend. When did fun make you feel like you had a hollow the size of the Pacific Ocean in your stomach?

She stomped back out of the tack room, loosened Crackers head collar, and slipped on his bridle. It was two days since she'd arrived home. *Two very long days. Long enough to seem like two weeks.* Soon she was going to have to stop going over everything in her head. Obviously someone as hunky as Ed Mitchum would never have looked at her under normal circumstances, without the inducement of a bet. She didn't know who she was the most furious with – him for the whole bet fiasco, or herself for going along with it. And the worst thing was she'd actually let herself have a good time. Enough of a good time for it to be hurting like mad now it was over.

'Steady now.'

Gritting her teeth, she pulled a handful of mane through Cracker's bridle. She only had herself to blame. Ed had made it perfectly clear from the outset that he was there for short term fun. What part of that had she not understood? The bet part was degrading, but the rest was her fault. There'd been the hot sex, and wow, it had been hot. She'd left here thinking she was frigid, and discovered she had the capacity of a sex bomb. So all that was good. She really didn't have anything to complain about. The joke was, at the time she was sure she'd kept her distance emotionally, thought she'd pulled off the no-strings thing no problem. But now, however much she tried to stop it, mental pictures of Ed Mitchum plagued her, day and night. There was no room for a man in her life at the best of times, and definitely not now. Yet here she was, feeling like the world was about to end. Entirely ridiculous too, when you'd bolted away from the guy in question. Doubly ridiculous when you knew he'd gone on an extended business trip to South America, most probably to get away from you. It didn't make any sense, which was why she kept going over and over it.

'No need to paw the ground, Cracker, I'll grab the saddle, and we'll be off.' She'd just bobbed back into the tack room, when she heard footfalls in the yard.

'Anyone there?'

Her heart lurched in her rib cage, and thumped into her throat.

Shucks. For a moment there she thought it was Ed. Something about the deep growl. Stupid. She took a breath in the gloom. Once her pulse rate slowed again, she'd go to see who it was.

'Millie?' A shadow filled the doorway, impossibly broad shoulders blocking the light.

What then..? Only one man she knew whose chiseled cheekbones would show up like that in the gloom.

'Ed...' Gawping now, as she noticed a carrier bag rammed under his arm, but her ability to form words had gone.

'Hey. Nice shorts.' He eased to lean against the door frame.

Nice shorts? Was that all he could say? She dodged to see his face better against the light, then wished she hadn't, when the view of his jaw made her knees sag.

Indignation brought her tongue back to life. 'I thought you were supposed to be in South America.'

Damn. Over the clatter of her heart beat hammering in her ears, she knew her voice sounded shaky. She swallowed down the butterflies battering to escape from her chest. One glimpse of him should not make her this excited.

'Ah, South America got shelved.' He shifted a little shamefacedly, then pushed the bag towards her. 'I brought you your parcel. It got separated from the rest of your things, and it arrived on my desk this morning.'

'I see. Thanks.' Dropping the saddle and the hat she was holding, she took the bag from him, biting back her disappointment as her chest deflated. Of course he hadn't come because he wanted to see *her*. How could she have been so stupid as to think that?

'And I came to say sorry too. I wasn't sure you'd even see me, after what I did. I shouldn't have involved you in the dating challenge, it was low, and I'm ashamed.' One rueful smile slid onto his face.

Millie grimaced as she warmed to the smile, wishing she didn't

186

feel so susceptible. No way was she going to let him know how awful she felt. 'Whatever. Thanks for the apology though.'

'I may be digging a hole for myself here, but I'm glad the whole bet thing happened. And I'm not excusing my behavior, but I wanted to tell you, for the record, that everything I did with you for the challenge, I did because I wanted to do it. Finding you injured in the field was just the start. The way you jumped me...' He broke off, his face crinkling into a mischievous grin.

'I didn't jump you!' She wasn't letting him get away with that one. 'You started it if you remember, trying to give the kiss of life to someone still alive.'

'Have it your own way, call it what you like, but that was one hot snog you gave me. By the time we'd been to the hospital and I'd looked after you for the night, popped in on you a few times, I was a long way through the tasks Will and Cassie had set out for me. You have to remember I've never spent so much time with one woman. And it may have sounded bad to you, but what you need to know is, the more I was with you, the more I wanted to be with you. I asked you to come to Provence because I had to go, and I didn't want to be there without you. When you think about it like that, I'm hoping it doesn't sound so bad. I guess I'm hoping that you might forgive me.' He inclined his head, resting it against the door frame, eyeing her hopefully.

She sighed, wishing the pleading in his eyes didn't make her tummy hurt so much. 'Maybe...'

'I'm actually pleased it happened. I'm even pleased you balled me out, and ran off.'

'Sorry?'

Where exactly was he going with this? So like a man to make a bad thing positive.

'I'm happy, because it shocked me to my senses.' He gave a shrug. 'There was this awful ache when you weren't there, like I'd

187

chopped my arm off or something. I guess that ache was what finally made me know I'm in love with you.'

'What..?' Millie screwed up her nose.. Had he just said..?

'I meant to stay away longer.' He narrowed his eyes, as if assessing her reaction. 'To give you time to calm down, time to see how *you* felt. Then the parcel arrived on my desk, and I couldn't stay away any more. The thing is, now I'm here, I don't even need to ask, because I can read it in your eyes. You want to be with me too, don't you? All this crazy heat between us, it's because we're in love.' He shot her a grin that walloped her square in the gut.

As the 'L' word crashed to the ground, her already clattering heart started to race...

'I need to be with you Millie. I don't care where, I don't care how. Here, London, South America, in a castle, in a tent, I don't give a damn, so long as we can be together.'

Open mouthed, she gulped back her panic, barely hearing what he said now, as an axe of pain cleaved through her chest. This beautiful guy, who she was aching to be with, was telling her he loved her, and wanted to be with her. And here she was, the last woman on earth who could ever have a right to be with him. She pulled in a ragged breath.

He reached out, rubbed a thumb across her cheek. 'Millie, you're crying.'

Tugging her towards him, his strong arms enveloped her, and as her head hit his chest she was engulfed by the familiar scent of clean clothes and hot-blooded man.

The man she couldn't have.

Choking on her sobs she squirmed out of his grasp, and pushed her way out of the tack room, blinking as she stumbled into the sunlight.

She had to run, run as far away from Ed as she could, for both their sakes.

She hurled herself towards the pony, untied him, scrabbled onto his back and with a swift squeeze of her legs she urged him up the drive, and out onto the road.

***

'Millie, don't forget your hat...'

Ed strode into the yard in time to see Millie, blond hair flying behind her in a haze, galloping off up the road on Cracker.

Not again. He shook his head, breaking into a run as he headed towards his car. Damn that he'd parked at the top of the drive – so she wouldn't see him arriving and leg it. He gritted his teeth. Millie running for the hills was getting to be a habit – twice in three days – but this time she wasn't angry, this was different. He'd read the hurt in her eyes. He threw himself into the driver's seat, flung the car into a three point turn, and screamed off after Millie.

Who'd have thought love would be so difficult? He barely knew if he was blazing with Millie for being so reckless, or scared witless in case something happened to her. Great. He blew in relief, as he caught a glimpse of her in the distance behind a dry stone wall, turning off the road and into the lane leading to the quarry. At least there shouldn't be any blasting today. Swinging the onto the quarry track, the car groaned and bounced as it bowled over the ruts. He was gaining on Millie now. Ahead of him, she was off the pony, now, pushing her way through the gate into the field above the quarry.

By the time his car had screeched to a halt, and he'd flung himself over the gate, Cracker was galloping up the field towards the brow of the hill. Not giving much for his chances of catching her, but he'd let her go in London, and no way was he going to give up this time. Flinging himself at the incline he began to run.

Ahead of him, Cracker and Millie were breaking the skyline now, silhouetted against the blue. Ed froze, as he saw Cracker rear up. Then his stomach hit the deck. Millie was falling.

His lungs were bursting as he powered on up the hill, fighting to reach Mille, who was sprawled on the grass ahead of him. Grimacing at the irony of the déjà-vu, dying inside as the image of Millie lying prone and deathly flashed through his mind. And then he was there, one hand on her honey-brown thigh, the other brushing back a hayrick of hair to find her jaw set, her smokey eyes sparking straight into his.

'Don't say it Mitchum.'

'What, the bit about girls who leave their hats behind not having any brains, or the I love you part?' He knew he was pushing it, but, what the hell, she was alive.

'The brains thing.' And showing her displeasure by kicking him.

He flinched as she caught him square on the shin. 'Whoa.'

Then her eyes blurred, and her voice sank to a whisper, 'About the other –' Her head rolled sideways as she avoided his gaze. 'There's stuff I need to tell you.'

He fought the urge to crash his mouth over hers.

'If its stuff that makes you tear off on horseback, maybe we'd better talk about it right away, if your head's okay that is?'

'My head's fine, it's my backside and my pride that are suffering.' She gave a shamefaced grimace 'A rabbit jumped up under Cracker's nose, I shouldn't have come off.' She pushed herself to standing, and hobbled towards the pony, grazing nearby, and knotted his reins. 'He's all good for a few minutes.' She eased herself down onto the grass again, drawing her legs in up front of her, and hugging her knees tightly.

'So?' He sat down beside her. 'If it's the money thing, I'll give it all away.'

'If only it were that simple. It's the love thing – it can't happen.'

She shook her head, disconsolately. She hesitated, drawing in a deep breath. 'When I told you your mother was strong when she decided to have you, I knew that because I went through the same thing as she did. Except I...' She faltered. 'I wasn't strong like your mother. I was weak and I was a coward, and everything went wrong.'

'Ah, Millie...' He reached to slide a protective arm around her, but she pushed him away.

'I regret it every day.' She blurted the words dismally, hanging her head. 'I was with Josh, at the end of my second year at uni. I told him I was pregnant, and he didn't want to know...'

'I knew he was a waste of space, I knew he'd hurt you.' Fire flared in Ed's belly at the mention of Josh. He'd always wanted to tear the guy limb from limb.

Millie sniffed, and swallowed hard. 'After my first scan at twelve weeks I started getting stomach cramps, and the doctor said I was over-tired and needed to rest. Oh, and to stop my dancing and strenuous exercise. So I ended up going home to my parents, which wasn't what I'd planned, but I didn't know what else to do. But once I got there, everyone started saying I wouldn't cope on my own, and questioning whether I should even go through with the pregnancy. I was already stressed, but their reaction was such a shock it made it worse. I can't blame anyone but myself, but we had this big argument, and I went dashing out of the house. It was raining, and I was down by the river, half running, half walking, when the cramps came on really badly, and I collapsed. Someone stopped and took me to hospital, but I was bleeding badly by the time I got there, and two days later I lost the baby. And it was all my fault. If I hadn't stressed my body like that, if I'd only stayed at home, who knows, the baby would have been okay.' She leaned back, raking her hands through the tangle of her hair, and sighed hopelessly.

'Don't be so hard on yourself, Mille, you don't know that'

'And the time in hospital was awful.' She screwed up her face, and shuddered. "That's why I couldn't bear to stay in hospital when I hurt my head. The smell of the antiseptic brought it all back.' Her bottom lip juddered, and she scraped away a silent tear.

'Sweetheart...' He reached across. At least she might let him hold her knee.

'The worst thing was, poor Sophie had been trying to have a baby for years. I think my parents couldn't bear to think of Sophie go through the agony of seeing me have an unplanned child when she couldn't have one herself.'

'Everyone tries to do their best in these situations, sometimes it's hard...'

Wanting to wrap her in his arms and hold her to make the hurt go away, but again she pulled away, as if she had to emphasise her separation.

'Sophie got pregnant shortly afterwards, and the full impact of what I'd done only hit me when Bella was born. That was when I decided to cut myself off from my family. I couldn't face seeing Bella growing up, and always being reminded of my mistake. And I had to learn to make my own decisions, and take responsibility for my own life, not go running back to my family, getting into arguments. So that if anything like that happened again, it would be down to me.'

'It hasn't has it?' *Millie pregnant?* 'Happened again I mean?'

'No, no.' She sounded quietly dismissive. 'I had an implant to make sure I never got pregnant again – not that I slept with anyone. There was never a danger of a pregnancy with us, the condoms were for health, not contraception.'

That put him in his place. Firmly. 'But then I made you go and see Sophie because I wanted to help you get over your jealousy, as a payback for how you helped me. How awful is that? I'm so sorry, making you see Bella like that. I even handed her to you.

192

That must have been terrible'

Talk about crashing his big feet in it.

'I practically expired when you dropped her on my knee, but in a way I think it helped. Now Bella's older, she's a person, an individual, not just a baby, and seeing her the other day made me appreciate that. I need to thank you for making me go there – I went back to Sophie's when I ran off from you, and I'd never have done that otherwise.' She sliced him a half smile.

First of the day, gratefully accepted, even if it was watery.

'But why does any of this get in the way of me loving you?'

She hugged her knees tighter.

'You of all people Ed deserve better than someone who did what I did. We both know that.'

'Hey, I'll be the judge of what I need. As I see it, you've taken me, a guy who was incapable of forming any kind of lasting relationship, who was very set in their bad-boy ways, and turned my life around. I was hell bent on introducing you to the joys of no-strings encounters, but you shook me up, made me see the world as a different place. You taught me how to trust, and you made me want to care.'

He broke off, but Millie only rubbed a hand across her nose, snapped off a blade of grass, and rolled it between her fingers.

'Then there was my mother. Without you, I'd still be hating her for something she wasn't responsible for.' He bobbed, trying to make her look at him. 'You showed me how to enjoy life Millie, in a way I never have. But most of all you taught me how to fall in love.'

'Maybe...' She gave a shrug, wiggled her feet, bit her thumb.

He had to be getting through to her.

'When you weigh all those things against what you're talking about, I'm sorry, but whatever you did in the past, right now you've earned my love fair and square.'

Finally she inclined her head towards him, and he caught the shine of tears on her cheek. Her lips were curled into a smile, and he dared to sneak an arm around her shoulder. This time she didn't pull away.

'So we're good then?'

As she answered with a nod, he closed his mouth over hers. It was a long time and a load of sweetness later, when he broke the kiss. And that was only because there was something he had to say.

***

Millie's head spun, as Ed pulled away.

Heady, dizzy, and in love, with the most glorious guy in the world, and letting his chocolate voice slide over her. Then he shot her a grin, as wide as an ocean, flipping her tummy one more time.

'It was seeing you with Bella that finally made me realise I was in love with you. I had this huge desire for you to have my children, which hasn't gone away, but I'll work with you on this one.' His shamefaced grimace melted into a smile. 'Although I'm hoping you'll marry me first? How do you feel about becoming Mrs Mitchum?'

Digging her fingers into his arms, to be sure this was real, she breathed in the wonderful scent of him

'Of course I'll marry you Ed.' Smiling, biting her lip, not knowing whether to laugh or cry, and ending up doing both.

'Thank you.'

He kissed her again, thoroughly, and she only broke away to rub a hand across her nose, hoping it wasn't running too much.

'You are one fast mover, for a confirmed bachelor who doesn't date.'

'Correction, I didn't date until you came along, and fell at my feet in this field. After a kiss as hot as the one you gave me that day, I'd have had to come back to find you again, challenge, or no challenge.' He brushed his thumb over her cheekbone, pushed away a tear. 'I think I probably fell in love with you the first time I saw you, lying there, and unconscious right here. And as I said earlier, I'm so glad you jumped me...'

His lips were twitching into a teasing smile, but she couldn't let that go.

'I told you before, I didn't jump you!'

'Bingo! I love it when you pout like that. And if you didn't jump me here, you definitely did it in the tent in Provence. High heels, lacy shorts and a jacket with no shirt under, doesn't give a guy any other option -- not this guy, with you the shorts, anyway.'

She laughed at him, her heart infusing with warmth. 'You are one bad boy Ed Mitchum.'

'Funny when you think, an explosion started all this off. Just proves your Big Bang Theory was right.'

'I thought that theory was about getting the bang out of the way in one date, not about sticking around long enough to get married.' Her eyes locked on Ed's tanned fingers, draped over her shoulder, and the base of her stomach shifted with desire, at the thought of what Ed did to her in the tent, and would do to her again.

'Now it's all about how love makes the big bangs last forever. And talking of big bangs, Future Mrs Mitchum, how about we take that pony home, so I can take you to bed – or the courtyard if you'd prefer to be alfresco.' He raised his eyebrows in her direction, twisted his mouth into another wicked smile that told her he knew he was letting himself in for a storm. 'And if your bruised butt is up to it, maybe you can give me that twirl on your pole?'